JUST A WISH AWAY

By

Barbara Freethy

JUST A WISH AWAY

(Cover by Adazing Design)

PublishingServices: www.klfpub.com

For information contact: barbara@barbarafreethy.com

PRAISE FOR THE NOVELS
OF BARBARA FREETHY

Also available from

Barbara Freethy

In the WISH SERIES

A Secret Wish (#1)

Booklist Available
www.barbarafreethy.com

JUST A WISH AWAY

Prologue

Fifteen years earlier...

"Race you to Dragon Rock," Braden Elliott challenged.

Twelve-year-old Alexa Parker barely heard him. Her attention was focused on the pile of pebbles and shells that had washed ashore. She was looking for tiny shards of sea glass or mermaid tears, as the locals called them. The Sand Harbor Beach on the coast of Washington State was known for the glass that the sea tossed up after years of being tumbled and turned by the waves and the salt water, finally landing on the sand as beautiful, colorful gems. When she grew up, she wanted to become a glassmaker, turn all those broken pieces into something amazing.

"Come on, Alexa," Braden urged.

She looked up at him, her determination wavering as she stared into his beautiful green eyes, that sometimes reminded her of the glass she collected. Braden had grown three inches over the summer, now towering over her at nearly six feet. His brown hair was thick and wavy and messed up by the wind. He was so cute; sometimes she just couldn't stop looking at him.

They'd known each other since they were ten, but this was the first summer she'd looked at him as more than just a friend. In fact, her stomach did a little flip flop every time he smiled at her. She didn't really know what to do about her new feelings. Part of her wanted to say something and the other part of her was just too scared. A couple of her friends had boyfriends, but she wasn't sure she was ready, and she only saw Braden in the summer.

While Braden lived at Sand Harbor year round, she only came for holidays and summers. Every June, she and her mom packed up the car and left Seattle to stay with her Aunt Phoebe at the beach. Her dad would come down on Thursdays and take long weekends in July and August. It was the perfect way to spend the summer.

She'd met some of Braden's Sand Harbor friends over the years, but when she was in town it was mostly just the two of them. They would meet up every morning on their bikes and take off to explore one of the three beaches that dotted the coastline. They'd search for sea glass, fly kites, build sand castles and make up stories about the people who vacationed in the big houses along the bluff. Sand Harbor was a quiet fishing village in the winter, but in summer, the town filled up with tourists and celebrities looking for a summer escape. Every year there seemed to be new houses being built along the bluffs.

"Alexa," Braden said impatiently. "You're daydreaming again."

It was a bad habit of hers, but one that didn't usually make him mad. Braden put his hands in the pockets of his jeans and stared out to sea, and she realized Braden's bad mood was more about his dad than about her. Braden's father was a soldier in the Army, and he was supposed to have come home by now, but they kept postponing his release date. Now they were talking about Christmas. Braden seemed to grow more worried with each passing day, and she knew that deep down he was afraid that his dad would never come home.

Wanting to cheer him up, she got to her feet. "Okay, I'll race you," she said. Making Braden smile again seemed more important than finding glass to add to her collection.

Her words did make him smile and no wonder. Braden loved action, running, biking, hiking. He hated to stand still.

She tossed the few pieces of glass she had collected into her backpack.

"I'll carry it for you," Braden said, taking the pack out of her hands. "I don't want you to say the backpack slowed you down."

"Fine." Braden would beat her whether she was carrying anything or not. She couldn't keep up with his long legs.

"And I'll give you a head start," he added.

She didn't bother to say thanks, just took off down the beach. She didn't like to run as much as Braden did, but there were times like this afternoon when it felt good to have the wind in her hair and the sun on her face. She was going to miss summer, and she was going to miss Braden.

Moisture filled her eyes. She hadn't told him yet about the change in plans. She hadn't wanted to ruin the day, but as the sun sank down to meet the sea she knew she was almost out of time.

Braden passed her, his stride long and easy, as if he wasn't making any effort at all, and he probably wasn't. He was a born athlete.

By the time she got to the rock that looked like a dragon, Braden was sprawled on the sand, a satisfied smile on his face.

She flopped down, breathless, her cheeks warm from the sun and the run.

Braden gazed at her with an odd expression in

his eyes. Her heart skipped a beat.

He looked like he wanted to kiss her.

Surprise and nervousness flared. She'd never kissed a boy, but she wanted to kiss Braden. She just didn't know how to get from where she was to where he was. There had to be at least three feet between them.

"You're staring at me," she said, licking her suddenly dry lips.

"You're – pretty."

Her heart skipped another beat. "I am?"

"You know you are." His jaw tightened, and then he jumped to his feet. "Hey, what's that?" He took off, jogging toward the base of the cliff.

She got up more slowly, disappointed that nothing had happened. Her friend at home, Colette, had already kissed two boys. Braden had said she was pretty, but maybe she wasn't pretty enough. She always freckled in the summer, and her fair skin was more likely to burn than tan. Her blonde hair was pulled back in a ponytail, because it tangled so easily in the wind. It certainly wasn't thin and silky like Colette's. And she didn't have on any make up, because her mother wouldn't let her wear more than lip gloss, even though she was in middle school.

No wonder Braden hadn't kissed her. He was one of the most popular boys in Sand Harbor. There were always girls calling out to him when they rode into town. She'd always felt a little special that she was the one he was with. But maybe that's because she liked to explore and was more of a tomboy.

"Alexa, come on," Braden said impatiently.

She walked over to join him. "What?"

"Look." He pulled out a sparkly, oddly shaped blue glass bottle from the sand. They'd found bottles before, but nothing like this. It appeared very old and unusual, like it had come from a shipwreck. "Wow," she murmured, dropping to her knees beside him. She took the bottle from him and spun it around, the blue turning to purple and red in the dusky light. "It's beautiful."

"You could break it apart and mix it with your other glass and make something amazing."

"Oh, no, I couldn't break this apart. Look at the colors. They're -- magical."

"Magic doesn't exist."

"It does if you believe."

"Well, I don't believe."

"Why not?"

"Because I don't," he said with a frown. "It's stupid. Magic is just about tricks."

"Not real magic," she argued. "Not miracle kind of magic."

He rolled his eyes.

"This could be a genie's bottle," she said, her imagination taking hold as she spun the glass in her hands. The colors created a kaleidoscope, a fast-moving rainbow, unlike anything she'd ever seen. She glanced over at Braden, who still had an expression of disgust on his face, but behind that stubborn glint in his eye was a hint of hope. And she fed on that hope. "If we pull out the cork, a genie might appear, and then we'll get to make a wish," she said.

"Yeah, right."

"You should try to believe."

"Why?"

"Because if you don't try, it might not work. And I want to make a wish. It's important to me."

"It's just a bottle, Alexa. It doesn't matter if you make a wish or not, because it won't come true."

She ignored him, her fingers tightening on the cork. There was something so compelling about the bottle that she couldn't believe it was something ordinary. There was no label on it, nothing to suggest what had once been inside, or might still be inside. It felt light, empty, but the glass was so thick, it was impossible to be sure. So she pulled the cork. It didn't budge. She tried again, but she couldn't move it.

"Give me that," Braden said. He grabbed the bottle and yanked out the cork.

As he did so, a spray of water hit her right in the face. She gasped at the unexpected wave that had hit the beach so close to them. They were yards away from where the tide usually hit. Wiping the salt water from her eyes, she stared at Braden. "What was that?"

"Just a wave," he said, running a hand through his damp hair. But there was an odd look in his eyes.

The air around them was suddenly misty. Where had the fog come from? Just minutes ago it had been sunny. She shivered, as the bottle seemed to glow between them. She waited for some figure to appear, but nothing happened.

"There's no genie," Braden said, an unexpected note of disappointment in his voice.

She took the bottle out of his hands. The glass was warmer than it had been. "Let's wish anyway," she said, feeling as if it were suddenly very important.

"Alexa –"

"Please, Braden. You have to put your hand on the bottle, too."

"I still think this is stupid."

"I understand. But do it anyway."

After a brief hesitation, he put his hand on the bottle, his fingers covering hers.

She didn't know if the magic was in the bottle or in his touch, but she felt hot all over.

Closing her eyes, she thought for a moment, and

then silently whispered...

"I wish Braden would fall in love with me."

The wish scared her a little. She didn't really understand love. She just knew she wanted to feel it. And she wanted Braden to feel it, too.

Opening her eyes, she caught Braden gazing back at her. She hoped he couldn't see the wish in her eyes. She'd feel so dumb. "What did you wish for?" she asked.

"I can't tell you."

"We tell each other everything," she protested.

"Not wishes," he said.

"Did you really make one?" she asked suspiciously.

He grinned. "That's for me to know and you to find out."

"Sometimes, I hate you," she said, hoping he'd never guess what her wish was.

With the fog hitting the beach, the sky had grown very dark. It was getting late, and she had no more time in which to stall.

"I have to tell you something," she said.

"What's that?"

"We're leaving tomorrow."

His jaw dropped and a frown turned down his lips. "Summer isn't over for two more weeks."

"I know, but my mom says we have to go."

"Why?"

"My parents aren't getting along."

"What else is new?" he asked. "They never get along."

"Well, it's worse now. They got into a huge fight last night. My dad slammed out of the house, and he didn't come home until this morning. He barely said anything to anyone, just packed up his stuff and left. My mom says we have to go back to Seattle so she can talk to him."

"Why doesn't she go by herself?"

"She said it's almost the end of summer anyway. I told her I wanted to stay, Braden, but she wouldn't listen. She was crying all night. I could hear her from my room after I went to bed. She's so angry and so sad."

"That sucks."

She let out a sigh. "Yeah, it does."

He stared at her for a long minute, his expression unreadable. "When are you coming back?"

"We usually come at Thanksgiving." Her stomach twisted into a knot as she realized how far away that was. She'd never worried before about Braden not being there when she came back for visits, but they were growing up, and it wouldn't be long before he got a girlfriend. He'd pick someone in town, someone who wasn't always leaving. And then where would she be?

"Thanksgiving, huh? That's not for months," he said heavily.

"I know. But we'll call and write, right?"

"Sure."

He didn't sound very convincing and lately she hadn't been able to read him as well as she used to.

"I guess we should go," she said. She wished she could make this day last forever, because she had a terrible fear that she might never see Braden again, that after today everything would change – unless her wish came true. She really needed a little magic right now. Everything else in her life was turning so dark.

As they walked across the sand, she told herself to stop getting so worked up. She would see Braden again. They were coming back in November. It was only a couple of months. But her mental pep talk did little to ease the tension in her body and the worry in her mind.

The lights were coming on in the houses above them, some casting long shadows on the sand, giving an eerie, almost surreal quality to the dusky evening. The big castle-like house that was one of her favorites was just in front of them, and she couldn't help looking up at the widow's walk, wondering if she would see the beautiful woman with the long red hair who often stood on the deck in a swirling white gown that made her seem almost like a ghost. She'd nicknamed her Ariel, because she reminded her of a mermaid.

Her heart skipped a beat as she saw the woman, but Ariel was definitely more alive than ghostly right now. She was shouting at someone – someone in the shadows.

Braden paused, too, his gaze moving upward.

"You lied to me," the woman shouted, her voice frenzied and filled with the pain of some betrayal.

Alexa couldn't hear what the other person said, but it did nothing to calm Ariel. She picked up something and threw it into the shadows. At the sound of a crash, Alexa moved a little closer to Braden, unsettled by the fight. While her parents hadn't resorted to throwing things at each other, they fought with the same kind of intense anger. She didn't understand how people could go from loving each other to hating each other.

"Don't tell me to be quiet," the woman yelled. "I'm tired of secrets. I can't keep it all in. I'm going to snap." She paused. "Don't touch me. I'll come in when I want to come in."

"We should go," Alexa said, her stomach feeling a little sick.

"Looks like she went inside anyway," Braden observed. "I wonder who she was arguing with and what all the secrets are about."

Normally, Alexa loved secrets, but not today. "I don't care. I just wish everyone would stop fighting. I hate when people yell at each other. It makes me feel sick to my stomach. How does love turn into hate?"

"It's going to be okay, Alexa."

"I wish I could believe that," she said as they started walking again.

"If you can believe in magic, you can believe in that," he said.

She sighed. "Maybe you're right. Maybe there is no magic."

He shook his head. "No, I don't want you to think that. I need you to believe."

"Why?" she asked, giving him a curious look.

His lips tightened and then he said, "Because then I can try to believe."

She gazed into his eyes and saw a need she could fulfill. "Then I will."

He nodded and they walked the rest of the way in silence.

When they reached their bikes, Braden handed over her backpack, and she put the genie's bottle inside.

"Do you want me to carry the backpack while you ride?" Braden offered.

"No, I can hang on to it," she said, slipping the straps over her shoulder. She didn't want to let go of the bottle, because when she got home, she was going to make another wish, a wish that her parents would stop fighting. It had occurred to her that she might have wasted her wish on her own chance at love, when what she should have been concentrating on was getting her parents back on the same page.

"Alexa," Braden said as she got on her bike.

"Yes?" she asked.

He moved his bike next to hers, then leaned over and kissed her on the mouth. His lips were firm and warm, a little salty, but actually quite perfect.

Before she could really register the fact that she'd just gotten her first kiss, he pulled away.

His voice was a little gruff when he said, "Come back, Alexa, okay?"

"I will," she promised, her heart racing.

Then she got on her bike and followed him down the road, wondering how long it would be before she saw him again.

Chapter One

Present Day...

When Alexa Parker was twelve years old, two monumental events happened. She fell in love for the very first time, and her parents got divorced. Alexa couldn't think of one event without the other. Now, returning to Sand Harbor as a twenty-seven-year-old adult, she was reminded of both.

Every street in the picturesque beach town seemed to hold a memory, the rocky path to the beach that she and Braden had ridden their bikes down every day, the Boardwalk with the cotton candy and hot pretzel carts that were crowded with kids in the summer, the fishing boats coming into the harbor after a long day at sea, Nini's Pancake House, where her dad used to take her on Sunday mornings, and the majestic houses on the bluffs that she'd dreamed about one day living in.

Like so many of her childhood dreams, living in a big house on her favorite beach was one that had fallen by the wayside. The same was true for her dream of becoming a glassmaker, of turning beautiful pieces of sea glass into something amazing, and also her dream of marrying her best friend. But those had been the dreams of an idealistic girl, who'd thought everything in life would always be perfect, exactly like that perfect summer kiss from Braden the very last time she'd seen him.

She was a different person now. She could barely remember that naïve girl, but she'd never forgotten her first kiss.

Unfortunately, her relationship with Braden had not lasted past that summer. Her parents' divorce had changed her life in every possible way. She and her mom had moved back East, far away from the Washington coast. Her dad had ended up in Los Angeles a few years later and had remarried and had other children.

The first few years she'd tried to keep in touch with Braden, but she'd had her hands full dealing with her mom's extreme depression and the move to a new city and a new school. Sand Harbor had seemed very far away. Their contact had faded to occasional calls and emails and then eventually nothing.

Braden had had his own problems to deal with, including the death of his father, who'd been killed in action when Braden was fifteen. She'd tried to get in touch with him then, but he'd never called her back. Her mother said she couldn't afford to fly her across the country for the funeral. That was pretty much the end of their tenuous relationship.

Years passed, and she dated other guys, but she was never quite able to get Braden out of her mind. Thinking she'd give it one more shot, she'd gone to Sand Harbor right after her college graduation. She was too late. She was shocked to learn that Braden had married at twenty, just weeks before enlisting in the Army.

The dream of her heart was finally shut down. Braden was taken. He was with someone else. She had to move on with her life.

That had been six years ago.

Now she was back in Sand Harbor, and she had no idea where Braden was, but it didn't matter. She wasn't here for Braden, she was here for her aunt, Phoebe Gray, who had been injured in a break-in at her antique store. While Alexa had been kept away from everyone connected to her father's side of the family, she had reunited with her father's older sister, Phoebe, on her last visit to Sand Harbor.

They'd been in frequent contact since then, a fact she'd happily kept from her mother, who was still quite bitter about that side of the family. But Alexa didn't blame her aunt or her uncle or her cousins for her parents' divorce. And she'd enjoyed getting to know them again over the past few years. Most of the contact was over email or through online social sites, but it was a start. When her cousin, Evie, had called her at dawn to tell her about the robbery, she'd immediately said she was on her way. She hadn't always been there for her aunt, but she could be there now.

She'd caught the first plane out of San Francisco, rented a car, and made the two-hour drive from Seattle to Sand Harbor. She'd stopped at the hospital first, but her aunt was unconscious, and the doctor said it could be hours before she woke up. Several of Phoebe's friends were in the waiting room, so reassured that her aunt would not be alone when she woke up, Alexa had decided to track down Evie and see what was happening with the police investigation.

Pulling into a spot down the street from her aunt's antique shop, aptly named Yesterday Once More, she drew in a deep breath and then stepped out of the car. The store was one of many boutiques on a downtown side street. Although, there was some foot traffic, there weren't quite as many tourists on this block. The shop sat between a vintage clothing store and a beauty salon. A small walkway separated the antique shop from the salon; a path many used to cut through to the main post office on the next block.

As Alexa approached the shop, she was again assailed with memories. Her aunt had opened Yesterday Once More thirty years ago, and almost everyone in the family had worked there at some time or another, herself included. She'd loved helping out in the store on her summer vacations. Like her aunt, she was captivated by anything that was old and came with a story. Imagining where the pieces had come from and who had used them had been one of her favorite pastimes.

Her gut tightened as she reached the shop. The big bay window was intact, but the glass over the front door had been shattered and was now boarded up with wood. Remnants of yellow crime scene tape clung to the frame. She still couldn't believe someone had broken into the shop. There had not been a lot of crime in Sand Harbor when she was growing up, but perhaps things had changed.

Seeing someone inside the shop, she tried the doorknob, but it was locked, so she knocked. A moment later, a woman's face peered around the corner of a large desk in the front window. Alexa waved, recognizing her cousin's dark brown hair and pretty blue eyes. Evie was the oldest daughter of her father's brother, Stan.

"Alexa," Evie, said with a relieved smile, as she opened the door. "I'm so glad you came."

Alexa gave Evie a hug and then glanced around the crowded showroom. Her aunt had always had plenty of inventory, but she'd also been very disciplined about keeping her displays organized. Now, everything was in chaos. Smaller items were strewn across the floor and on some of the tables and desks. There was broken glass as well as shattered tiles and ceramics on the floor. It looked as if the thief had been more interested in destroying the pieces rather than stealing them, but that didn't make sense.

"Wow," she murmured. "I had no idea it would be this bad."

Evie nodded, her lips drawing together in a tense line. "It's horrible."

"Have the police caught the person or people who did this?"

"Not yet. The Chief of Police, Edwin Hayes, actually found Aunt Phoebe. They're good friends, and he said he'd had a hunch she might be working late, so he'd stopped by. If he hadn't done so, it might have been morning before anyone found her. She'd already lost a lot of blood by the time the paramedics got there.

Alexa followed her cousin's gaze to the dark red stain on the floor by the front counter. Her stomach turned over as she realized how close her aunt had come to losing her life.

"They don't know if Aunt Phoebe was struck from behind or if she hit her head on the counter when she fell, but she has a big gash on the back of her head," Evie added.

"I saw the bandage around her head. I stopped by the hospital on my way here. She was asleep and surrounded by friends. I thought I might be of more help if I came here."

Evie nodded. "That makes sense. I'm going to stop by this evening. Aunt Phoebe's friend, Louise, promised to call me if there's any change." Evie paused. "I feel so bad about what happened. It's partly my fault."

"Why would you say that?" Alexa asked in surprise.

"I came by here yesterday afternoon. Aunt

Phoebe had just gotten in a big delivery from the Wellbourne estate, all those boxes," she added, pointing to a stack of eight to ten boxes, some of which were opened and upturned on the floor, some of which were still sealed. "She told me she was going to come back after dinner and get a head start on unpacking, because the weekends are so busy and she wanted to make room in the store before the tourists descended."

"You couldn't have predicted a robbery, Evie."

"No, but I knew she was going to be in the store late at night. I should have tried to dissuade her from coming in alone or persuaded her to wait until today. I also could have offered to help. Beverly Adams, Aunt Phoebe's assistant, is on vacation until next week."

"Evie, stop it. Aunt Phoebe wouldn't have been persuaded to wait even if you'd tried to talk her into it. This shop is her baby and she watches over it like a hawk. Besides that, she's stubborn."

"Stubbornness is a Parker family trait," Evie said with a sigh.

"Exactly."

"I'm so glad you were able to come, Alexa. My parents are in Europe right now, and I haven't been able to catch up with them yet, so I want to make sure I'm taking care of everything."

"I'll help you however I can." Alexa said.

"I appreciate that. Did you speak to your parents? Is your father coming?"

"I left a message for my dad, but he hasn't returned my call. That's not unusual. We don't talk often, especially since his wife had another baby."

"I can't believe your father is having babies at his age," Evie said, raising an eyebrow.

"His wife is fourteen years younger," she said,

deliberately keeping her tone neutral. She didn't want to get into her feelings about her dad's marriage. She should have been used to it all by now. It had been twelve years since he'd married his second wife, and this new baby was number four.

"And your mom?" Evie asked somewhat tentatively.

"She's actually the best I've seen her in years. She got remarried last year, and her husband is in the wine business. She often goes on trips with him, and she seems happy."

"I'm glad for her and for you."

"Thanks."

"Aunt Phoebe will be happy to see you when she wakes up."

Alexa liked the hopeful note in Evie's voice. She didn't want to think about the possibility that her aunt would never wake up. That was too awful to contemplate. "So what can I do?" she asked.

"If you want to start with clean up, that would be great. I have to pick up my twins from school in a few minutes, so I won't be able to do much more today. If you unpack anything, just make sure to write down each item with a brief description. Aunt Phoebe is a stickler for details."

"I remember that from when I worked here as a kid."

"Some things don't change," Evie said with a smile.

"So the shipment is from an estate?"

"The Wellbournes. They own that big house on the bluff."

"Oh, sure," she said. That house had served as the foundation for many a daydream, not only because it was enormous, but also because there had always been an air of mystery about it. She and

Braden had made up numerous stories about the people who had stayed there.

"Jack Wellbourne died last week, and left some of his antiques to Aunt Phoebe."

"That was nice of him."

"She was very excited to see what he'd left her. Apparently, he was quite a collector." Evie grabbed some keys off the counter and tossed them to her. "Lock up when you leave. In fact, you might want to keep the door locked until we're sure there won't be any more trouble." She paused. "If you'd rather not be here alone, we can leave this for later."

That was a tempting thought, but Alexa knew that her aunt would want the shop put back in order as soon as possible, and she had nothing else to do. It was broad daylight, and there were a number of people on the street, so she didn't feel in any danger.

"I don't mind cleaning up and getting some pieces inventoried," she said. "I might as well do something productive."

"If it makes you feel better, the police said they'd keep an eye on the shop for the next few days."

"That's good."

"Where are you staying?"

"I reserved a room at the Cheshire Inn."

"You could have stayed with us. Although, twin six-year-olds, two dogs and a cat make life a little hectic."

"But you're happy," Alexa said, seeing the sparkle of pride and love in Evie's eyes when she talked about her family.

"I am stressed a lot of the time, but life is still pretty wonderful." Her gaze softened. "It's good to have you here, Alexa. I hate what happened to our family. One minute we were all spending awesome summers and holidays together, and then you and your parents were gone. I missed you."

"I missed you, too."

"Did you miss anyone else? Like Braden Elliott?" Evie asked with a mischievous sparkle in her eye.

"Braden was my friend a long time ago."

"You two were inseparable that last summer you were here." Evie paused. "He's back, you know."

Her heart jumped. "Really? I thought he was serving overseas."

"He was until three months ago. Aunt Phoebe didn't tell you?"

"No, but I've been busy with tax season. We haven't been emailing lately." She cleared her throat. "Is Braden still in the Army?"

"I think he's done. He was injured in action several months ago. I don't know the details, but he was in a hospital for about two weeks before he came back here. I've only seen him once from a distance, and at the time he was using a cane. That was awhile ago."

Her throat tightened at the thought of Braden being hurt. "I'm sorry to hear that, but he has a wife to help him get through it."

Evie shook her head. "Not anymore. She asked him for a divorce before he was even out of the hospital."

"Are you serious? How could she do that to her injured husband?"

"She's a bitch from what I hear. I don't know her. But most people think she's pretty hard-hearted. Anyway, Braden rented an apartment and has been keeping to himself since he got home." She paused. "Maybe you should go by and see him."

"I don't think so," she said quickly.

"Why not?"

It was a good question. And the real answer was because she was scared. But she couldn't begin to explain her muddled thoughts to Evie. So she said, "Because we don't know each other anymore. I'm sure I'm the last person he wants to see right now. Braden is part of my past. He was a childhood crush, that's all. There's nothing between us now."

Evie shrugged and gave her a small smile. "Not yet anyway."

* * *

"You need to work, Braden. And I could use your help."

Braden rocked the wooden chair in his kitchen back on two legs, folded his arms across his chest, ignored the ache in his healing ribs and stared across the table at his longtime friend, Drew Lassen. Drew had gone from skateboarder to police officer, a path Braden had never foreseen his once wild and rebellious friend taking. But then they'd both changed a lot since their high school days. "I'm not a cop," he said simply. "And I don't need to work. I'm supposed to be resting."

"You've been resting, and you can't sit in this apartment all day every day." Drew glanced around the room, a frown spreading across his face as he took in the bare furnishings. "This place sucks."

"It's fine."

"It's depressing. You should have gone to your mom's house."

He shook his head. "The last thing I need is my mother hovering over me."

"Where's the rest of your stuff?"

"Kinley has it," he said shortly.

"You're being generous to a woman who doesn't

deserve it."

"There's nothing she has that I want anymore." As the words left his mouth, he realized just how true they were.

"Fine, but I've known you a long time, and you're not someone who just sits around."

"I'm recuperating, didn't you hear?" he asked, a cynical note in his voice as he remembered all the platitudes he'd been offered by the doctors who'd attended to him in recent months, as if time would heal all his wounds. That simply wasn't possible. Most of his wounds weren't physical.

"You look like you're ready to be back on your feet," Drew said.

"I'm sure you have enough manpower to keep the citizens of Sand Harbor safe," he said.

"Ordinarily yes, but two officers are out sick and another is on vacation. Plus, I need to provide extra security for Daniel Stone's fundraiser on Saturday night. He's launching his senate campaign here in Sand Harbor this weekend."

"Trying to remind the locals he was born here?" Braden asked cynically. Daniel Stone's parents owned a house in Sand Harbor, but the Stones were very wealthy and had homes all over the world.

"I don't care about his reason, just what it means for me – which is more security."

"I'm sure he can afford to hire his own security."

"Well, I don't need your help with Stone." Drew paused. "Did you hear about the break-in at Phoebe Gray's antique shop?"

"No," he said, his gut tightening at the mention of Alexa's aunt. No matter how many years passed, every time he saw Phoebe or heard something about her, he thought about Alexa.

"It happened last night," Drew said. "I'm

surprised no one told you."

"I haven't spoken to anyone." Since he'd returned home, his mother and sister had been driving him crazy, asking him every two seconds how he felt, whether he needed anything. He knew they were concerned, but he needed to be on his own for a while so he could sort out his life.

"Phoebe went down to her store last night and interrupted a robbery. She was knocked out and has a serious concussion."

He was shocked. "I can't believe it. Do you have any leads?"

"None. We've had some vandalism around town, but nothing to this extent, and certainly no one was assaulted in the previous incidents. We're hoping when Phoebe wakes up, she'll be able to give us some information, but until then, I'd like to get your help. You can use some of those investigative skills you acquired in Army Intelligence."

"Did you run this by your boss?" he asked doubtfully.

"I mentioned it to Chief Hayes. I made it clear that you would just be helping out on a peripheral level, and he was fine with it. He's good friends with Phoebe and he doesn't want to leave any stone unturned. He's also aware that we're shorthanded, and you have an excellent background for this kind of work. Plus, you're a local boy. People will talk to you."

"I don't know, Drew."

"Do you have something better to do?" Drew challenged.

"Obviously I don't," he said. "What exactly do you expect me to do?"

"Look around the store, see if we missed anything, ask some questions, talk to the other shop owners."

"I suppose I could do that," he said slowly. He liked Phoebe, and she was Alexa's aunt. He wondered if Alexa had heard about the robbery. He drew in a deep breath, just the thought of her unsettling him. It had been years since he'd let himself think about her for longer than a second. "I'll stop by there tomorrow."

"Go today," Drew said as he got to his feet. "Let me know if you find anything."

* * *

It was six o'clock and the May sky was starting to darken when Braden approached the antique store. He'd always liked twilight -- that in between time between day and night when everything seemed very still. It was a Wednesday evening and most of the shops closed up by five during the week.

He hadn't been in the antique store since he was a kid, probably not since that last summer he'd hung out with Alexa. She used to help her aunt on the weekends and occasionally he joined her, although he'd never been as interested in the antiques as she had been. She'd loved making up stories about the treasures they sold, and like always he'd gotten caught up in her imagination. She could take almost anything and spin it into a story so real he thought it had actually happened. He'd admired her ability to escape reality so easily. Unfortunately, her imagination had been honed by an unhappy home life. She'd told him that when her parents started fighting, she'd pull the covers over her head and make up stories where she was part of some big, happy family.

His household had been much happier, but his

father had been gone a lot. He was career Army, and they'd moved around a lot before his mom finally decided to settle in Sand Harbor where her family was. He'd met Alexa shortly after his arrival, and he'd connected with her instantly. The reality that his dad might not make it home had been with him constantly. It was that nagging worry that had made escaping into Alexa's stories even more appealing. They'd been quite a pair, sharing everything. He'd told her things he'd never imagined he'd say out loud, much less to another person.

A pang of nostalgia tightened his throat. Damn! He really didn't need this trip down memory lane. The last couple of months had been brutal, and he wasn't close to being a hundred percent in any part of his life.

But this wasn't about Alexa; it was about her aunt. If he could do anything to help find out who had put Phoebe in the hospital, he was more than happy to help.

There were lights on in the store, and through the front window, he could see someone moving around inside. The boarded-up door told him the break-in had been rough and unsophisticated. Maybe it had been some restless teenagers thinking it might be fun to vandalize the antique shop and hadn't realized anyone would come by after normal work hours.

He turned the knob, but the door was locked. Knocking sharply on the wood, he hoped one of Phoebe's assistants could give him more information about what had happened.

A moment later the door opened a few inches. A woman gave him a wary look. In the shadowy light, he thought his eyes were playing on tricks on him. But as the surprise flared in her blue gaze, his breath stopped.

Alexa!

She pulled the door all the way open, and for a moment all he could do was look at her. She was dressed in dark jeans, black boots, and a coral-colored sweater that hugged her curves. Her blonde hair was swept back from her face in a thick ponytail that hung past her shoulders. There was only a hint of the freckles that had once dotted her nose. Dark lashes framed her beautiful eyes and her light pink lips were soft and sexy.

Damn! She'd been a fantasy in his head for so long he could hardly believe she was real. He needed to catch his breath, find his voice.

But she beat him to it.

"Braden?" she said. "Is it really you?"

Chapter Two

Over the years, Alexa had dreamed of seeing Braden again. She'd imagined thousands of different scenarios where they just happened to run into each other, but none of those meetings had ever occurred. All afternoon, he'd been on her mind. Since learning that he'd been injured and was getting a divorce, she couldn't seem to think about anything else. She'd tried to convince herself that she'd be in and out of town so fast there wouldn't be an opportunity to reconnect with him. She'd told herself it would be best to leave the past alone. But here he was.

Braden had certainly grown up well. He was handsome and rugged in his worn jeans and long-sleeve, dark sweater that stretched across a chest much broader than she remembered. He'd also added a few more inches, towering above her now, and there wasn't an ounce of fat on him. His green eyes still lit up his face and his brown hair was thick and wavy. There was a scar on his chin and a day's growth of beard along his jaw. Weary lines edged his eyes and mouth. He'd lived a lot of life since she'd seen him last, and she imagined much of that life had been very difficult

"Alexa," he finally said, breaking the lengthening silence between them. "I didn't expect to see you. I didn't think you'd ever come back to Sand Harbor."

"My aunt is in the hospital."

"I heard. Is she all right?"

"I'm not sure. She's unconscious. The doctors think she'll wake up, but until she does, it's scary. I'm really worried."

He nodded, his lips tightening. "You must be. I can't believe someone broke into this place," he added, his gaze sweeping the cluttered showroom.

She'd been working a few hours and had barely made a dent in the chaos. She'd cleaned up the broken pieces and then started in on the boxes, but that was a slow process. She had to write detailed descriptions of every piece and then find somewhere to put the piece, which wasn't easy. Her aunt seemed to have a large inventory at the moment. It had obviously been a slow winter for antique sales.

"When did you get in?" Braden asked.

"This afternoon. My cousin, Evie, called me just after six this morning to tell me what happened, and I got on the first plane."

"The first plane from where?"

"San Francisco. I've been there three years now."

"I didn't realize. I thought you were still back East."

"I was tired of the snow." She wondered how long they could continue to exchange meaningless conversation. But while she was tempted to go deeper, she was also wary.

Braden tilted his head, his expression turning thoughtful. "I didn't think you kept in touch with your aunt."

"We reconnected several years ago." She paused. "I came here after my college graduation."

Surprise flared in his gaze. "You did?"

"Yes. I missed my aunt and the rest of my family." She couldn't possibly tell him she had missed him, too, and that he'd been one of the reasons she'd made the trip.

"Maybe you should have come back earlier," he suggested, a hard note in his voice. "There were people here who cared about you."

"I couldn't." Seeing the skepticism in his eyes, she repeated the words more firmly. "I couldn't, Braden. I was a kid. My mother moved me across the country. I had no way of getting back here. And even if I had, I probably wouldn't have taken it until after college, because my mom was a mess. I was all she had left after the divorce, and she would have viewed my coming here as a betrayal. I couldn't do that to her."

"She can't be happy you're here now then."

"She doesn't know. But she probably wouldn't care anymore. She got married again last year, and she's finally found some happiness, and someone else to lean on." Alexa paused, sure she was about to make a big mistake, but she couldn't stop herself. "Do you want to come in?"

He hesitated. "I might as well. I'm here."

She stepped back to let him enter. "Why are you here?" she asked.

He glanced around the store, his sharp gaze taking in every detail. "Drew Lassen asked me to stop by. I don't know if you remember him."

"He was the kid who was always on a skateboard."

"Yeah, well, he's a cop now. He's investigating the break-in, and he asked for my help. The department is short-handed. I have some investigative experience from the Army, so ..." he shrugged. "I said I'd look around, ask some questions, but if you'd rather I wasn't involved –"

"No, it's fine," she said. "But I thought you were injured. Evie said earlier today that you'd been hurt."

"I'm better," he said shortly.

She wanted to ask him a dozen more questions including what had happened with his marriage, but he was moving toward the stack of boxes.

"What's all this?" he asked.

"It's a delivery from the Wellbourne estate. It came yesterday. Apparently, my aunt wanted to get an early start on the unpacking, so that's why she came back after hours last night." She paused as he opened one of the boxes. "Don't take anything out. I'm writing down a description of each piece before I put it away."

"Looks like a big job." He turned back to her. "How long are you planning to stay?"

There was an intensity behind his question, and she had no idea if he wanted her to stay or wanted her to go. His expression was difficult to read.

"I'm not sure," she replied. "It depends on how quickly my aunt recovers and what the investigation turns up."

"What about your job? Your life? You can just take off for a while?"

"I'm an accountant. It's slower now that we've passed April 15th. I have some time off."

His jaw literally dropped. "What did you say you do?"

She crossed her arms and shifted her feet, feeling defensive for no good reason. "I'm an accountant," she repeated. "Why are you looking at me like that, Braden?"

He shook his head in disbelief. "Because you can't be an accountant."

"It's a good job."

"It's a great job, but it's not you. You're the girl who wanted to make art out of sea glass, who told stories about dragons and nicknamed every person in town."

She frowned. "That was a long time ago. I was a kid then. You don't know me anymore, Braden."

"I guess I don't."

She didn't like the note of disappointment in his voice and felt the need to explain. "I grew up fast after we left here. My life fell apart and I had to find a way to put it back together. I had to be practical and responsible. There's not exactly a demand for glassmakers these days." She took a quick breath. "I like what I do, and I'm good at it."

"Okay," he said, putting up a hand. "It's your life."

"It *is* my life," she echoed. She wished she could say he'd changed, too, but he'd done exactly what she'd thought he would do. "You may be surprised by my choices, but I'm not surprised by yours, although I wondered why you didn't finish college before you enlisted."

"College seemed like a distraction. I knew where I needed to be, where I was always meant to be, so I signed up."

"And got married."

He flinched but he didn't avert his gaze. "Yeah, I got married."

"I couldn't believe it when I heard. You were so young."

"It seemed like the right thing to do at the time."

"Not anymore?"

"I'm sure your cousin filled you in."

"She just said she heard you were getting a divorce. I'm sorry."

"I'm not." He turned back to the stack of boxes. He pulled out a cigar case and gave it a thoughtful look. "I haven't seen one of these since my dad used to take me to the Smoke Shop. He loved cigars."

She hesitated for a moment, then said, "I was

sorry to hear about your dad, Braden. I tried to get in touch with you after he died, but you didn't return any of my calls or letters. I know you must have been devastated."

"It was a bad time. I wasn't in the mood to talk to anyone, Alexa."

"I figured, but I wanted to try."

"Why? We weren't friends any more."

"I guess I still thought we were," she said, feeling a little annoyed by his dismissive attitude.

"How could you think that? We hadn't talked in months."

"There were extenuating circumstances."

"Whatever. It doesn't matter anymore."

Judging by the tension between them, it seemed like it did matter, but she didn't think she would get anywhere by pointing that out.

Braden set the cigar case down and picked up a lamp with a hula dancer at the base. "Well, here's something worth stealing," he said sarcastically.

"There seems to be a mix of good and bad," she said.

"Looks like more bad to me. In fact, most of this is what I'd call junk."

She smiled to herself, his words drawing up an old memory. "You always used to say this whole store was full of junk. Aunt Phoebe would get so angry."

He glanced back at her. "And you always used to say I wasn't looking hard enough."

For the first time since he'd entered the shop, he actually cracked a small smile, and a tingle ran down her spine.

"I can't believe you remember that," she said.

He drew in a long breath. "I've tried to forget."

"Me, too," she whispered.

Their eyes met and held for a long moment. Heat rose within her, and she felt a little dizzy from all the tension and emotion. She put her hand on the counter as her legs suddenly felt weak.

"Are you all right?" Braden asked.

"It's been a long day, and I haven't eaten. It all just caught up to me." Not to mention the fact that her first love was now standing right in front of her.

"Can I get you something?"

She shook her head. "I'll eat when I leave."

"Are you staying at your aunt's house?"

"No, I got a room at the Cheshire Inn. It seemed easier."

"There's a Mexican restaurant just down the street from there, La Cantina. They make great enchiladas and even better margaritas."

She licked her lips, not sure he was inviting her to dinner or just making a suggestion. "That sounds good. I wonder if they do take-out. I don't like to eat alone in restaurants. I never know where to look. It feels so awkward." She paused. "Do you remember Mr. Penguin?"

"The old fat guy who always ate alone at Mack's Shack? Yeah I remember him. We watched him often enough."

"I guess we did." Mack's Burger Shack had been high on their list of summer eating adventures. It was on the beach and the burgers only cost a dollar on Tuesdays.

Another pause fell between them. Braden shifted his stance. "If you want to go together, I could eat."

It wasn't the nicest invitation she'd ever received, but it was a chance to spend more time with Braden, and now that they were together, she wasn't quite ready to let him walk away.

"I'd like that, but I need to check in with the

hospital first."

"No problem. Why don't I meet you there? I'll go by the police station and talk to Drew. Maybe he has more information on this new shipment from the Wellbournes."

"I'd appreciate that. Thanks." As Braden walked out of the shop, she let out the breath she'd been holding. Her entire body was tingling with a mix of excitement and nervousness. Everyone said you couldn't go home again. She had a feeling she was about to find out if that was true.

* * *

Braden left the antique shop wondering what the hell had just happened. A couple of hours ago he'd been sitting in his apartment, nursing a beer, and pondering the path his life had taken. Then Drew's offer had sent him not just to the antique store but straight back into his past. And now he'd invited Alexa to dinner.

He couldn't believe it. What was he thinking? He'd wasted most of his adolescence being obsessed with Alexa. It had taken far too many years to get her out of his head. He didn't need her back in it. He had enough problems.

But seeing the fear and worry in her eyes had brought out his protective instincts. He wanted to help her, to make everything all right for her, just the way he always had. Not that he'd been successful at that when he was twelve. Her problems had been too big for him to handle then. But now there was a chance he could actually help her, and he couldn't walk away. He just had to make sure that he didn't let himself get caught up in the fairytale that she'd spun around him a long time ago.

Many years had passed since they'd roamed the beaches of Sand Harbor. He was a different person now. That idealistic boy was long gone. Maybe it was a good thing they were going to dinner. The more time they spent together, the sooner they'd both realize that their past was not going to be their future.

Drew was on the phone when Braden arrived. He took a seat in the chair next to Drew's desk, noting the empty cubicles in the room. Drew hadn't been lying when he'd said they were short-handed, but Braden was still suspicious about his friend's motives. Since running in to Alexa, he couldn't help wondering if Drew had had another reason for asking for his help.

"Did you deliberately set me up?" he asked when Drew ended the call.

"What are you talking about?" Drew asked warily.

"You knew she was going to be there, didn't you?"

"Who?"

"Alexa," he said.

"Oh, right." Drew settled back in his creaky desk chair, crossing his arms. "I didn't actually know Alexa was in town when I saw you earlier. Evie told me that Alexa had arrived when I stopped by the hospital a short while ago. I was surprised Alexa was here. She hasn't been in Sand Harbor since she was a kid. I didn't think she kept in touch with her aunt."

"Apparently she does, and she's here."

Drew gave him a speculative look. "Does this mean you're out?"

He ran a hand through his hair, wishing he could say yes, because that would be the smart thing to do. Unfortunately, when it came to Alexa, he'd never been smart. "No, I'm not out. I'm going to dinner with her."

A light sparked in Drew's eyes and he smiled. "No kidding?"

"Don't get any ideas," he warned. "She practically fainted when I saw her. She needs to eat, and I'm hungry. So we're going to have a meal together. That's it."

"Maybe she fainted because she saw you," Drew suggested.

"That wasn't it," he said shortly. Although he'd been so caught up in his own reaction to her, he could barely remember what she'd first said to him. Ignoring the interested gleam in Drew's eyes, he changed the subject. "Have you learned anything new since we last spoke?"

"No. I was hoping you were here to give me a lead."

"Alexa told me her aunt received a substantial shipment from the Wellbourne estate yesterday. It seems like an interesting connection."

"I agree, but Jack Wellbourne lived alone in the beach house the last couple of years. If someone wanted something, why wait until the contents were delivered to an antique shop? They could have broken into the house at any time."

"That's true." But despite the logic of Drew's response, Braden wasn't completely sold. The timing of the delivery and the break-in seemed too coincidental, and he'd never been one to believe in coincidence. "What about other Wellbournes? Is there anyone in the family who might have wanted those items?"

"Jack divorced his second wife about six years ago, Roberta Wellbourne. She was a lot younger than Jack, by about fifteen years. She's now single and the campaign strategist for Daniel Stone. In fact, she came by the department yesterday afternoon to discuss security concerns for the fundraising event."

"So you spoke to her before the break-in?" It was interesting that Roberta had just arrived back in town.

"Yes, but she didn't seem to be revving up to rob the antique store," Drew said dryly. "It was all about politics. She was very concerned with making sure that Daniel gets a good launch here in Sand Harbor. Apparently, she's using her old Wellbourne ties to bring out the local money."

"Didn't Jack have some kids?"

"Two sons with his first wife, Laura. She passed on when his kids were little. The men are in their mid thirties now. I've contacted both of them. Neither one of them said they had any problems with the distribution of their father's belongings. They're both wealthy in their own right and apparently inherited a great deal of money, according to the lawyer I also spoke to. One of the sons told me he thought their father was in love with Phoebe, so it wasn't surprising that he left her some trinkets."

"It looked like more than a few trinkets," he said. "There are a lot of items. Did the attorney provide a list of what was shipped to the shop?"

"No, apparently the pieces were put in boxes some years ago and stored in the attic, each one marked for delivery to the store, but there was no itemized list."

"That doesn't help."

"No, it doesn't."

"Who found Phoebe and called for help?" he asked, as it occurred to him that there might be someone else to talk to.

"Edwin Hayes."

"The Chief of Police?" he asked in surprise.

"Yes. The Chief is a neighbor and a very close

friend of Phoebe's. They spend a lot of time together. She told him she was going to get a head start on the unpacking and after he got off work, he went by to help her. Unfortunately, he got there a little late."

"He didn't see anything or anyone?"

"No, and he knows how to review a crime scene. He made sure that we did a thorough sweep of the shop and the surrounding area. He is very determined to find out who did this. That's why he was all right with me bringing you in. And I'm glad I did." Drew paused, a knowing gleam in his eyes. "Because you're getting interested in this case. You're talking like an investigator."

"I always liked puzzles," he admitted.

"Especially when you were working them with Alexa," Drew pointed out.

"Don't start."

"So what does she look like? Better or worse than you expected?"

"I'm sure you'll see her," he said, getting to his feet.

"You're not going to give me anything?"

"No."

"Where are you going to eat?"

"La Cantina."　˅

"Watch the margaritas. They can be deadly, especially where hot blondes are concerned."

"I never said she was a hot blonde."

Drew laughed. "But she is, isn't she?"

He frowned. "Are you sure you didn't set me up?"

"I wish I'd thought of it. It would have been a hell of a good idea." Drew's expression turned more somber. "Kinley treated you like shit. After everything you went through, you didn't deserve –"

He cut Drew off with a wave of his head. "You

don't know what I deserved."

"You're going to defend Kinley?" Drew asked in amazement.

"She did what she had to do. And I'm doing what I have to do. Leave it alone." The last thing he wanted to think about was his marriage, especially right before he was going to see the one woman he'd always thought he'd marry.

Chapter Three

La Cantina was busy for a Wednesday night. There was a twenty-first birthday party, some singles chatting it up at the bar, and a dining room filled with families. Alexa put in her name with the hostess, snagged a stool at the less crowded end of the bar and ordered a margarita. She wasn't a big drinker, but tonight she needed something to take the edge off. It had been a long, emotional day, worrying about her aunt, seeing the destruction in the shop and then running into Braden again.

It was silly to be nervous about having dinner with him. This was the kid she'd shared peanut butter and jelly sandwiches with. But she couldn't deny the rapid beat of her pulse or her sweaty palms. Braden had grown up to be a very sexy, masculine man, and even if she hadn't known him as a kid, she would have been attracted to him. She couldn't imagine a woman that wouldn't be, although he might have to work a little on his charm. She wondered if he was that moody and angry with everyone or just with her. He'd definitely been tense during their conversation.

The bartender set down a very large margarita, and she took a grateful sip, enjoying the slide of the icy blend down her throat. Looking around the restaurant, she tried to distract herself by people watching. She wondered if any of the other patrons were people she'd known in her past, kids that had grown up to get married and have children of their own. But no one in the immediate vicinity looked at all familiar, until Braden walked in.

She drew in a quick breath, feeling like she'd taken another punch to the stomach.

"You got a head start," Braden said, joining her at the bar.

"I was thirsty."

"Sorry if I kept you waiting."

"You didn't. I just got here a few minutes ago."

"How's your aunt?"

"No change. She's still asleep. I ran into Evie at the hospital and a half dozen of my aunt's friends in the waiting room. They're pretty much doing a round-the-clock vigil, so if she does wake up, someone will be there. I always knew Aunt Phoebe was popular, but I didn't realize how many people are devoted to her. It's very impressive."

"Part of living in a small town. People care about each other. The flip side is that everyone wants to be in your business."

"We're not talking about my aunt any more, are we?" she said knowingly.

"No, we're not. Where is that bartender?" he muttered.

"Are people getting in your business, Braden?"

"They're certainly trying."

Before she could say more, the hostess called her name.

"We're up," she said.

"Great, I'm starving."

Alexa took her drink with her as the hostess led them to a table in the back of the restaurant. The young woman handed them some menus and told them their server would be with them in a moment. A busboy followed, dropping off chips and salsa and two glasses of water.

Alexa sipped her margarita, both relieved and

uncomfortable with the quiet. It would be easier for them to talk here, but did she really want to talk? Braden had been a shadowy image in her head for a long time. She didn't really know what to say to the real, live version of him. And he was touchy. She sensed it wouldn't take much to set off the smoldering fire in his eyes.

Braden suddenly put his hand over hers, stilling her rapidly drilling fingers.

Their eyes met.

He smiled. "Some things don't change."

The heat from his fingers warmed her all the way through – or maybe that was the tequila in her margarita. "Sorry, bad habit," she said, pulling her hand away.

"I remember."

"So this place wasn't here when I was a kid. It was something else," she said, changing the subject. "It was a diner, wasn't it?"

"With really bad food," Braden said. "It went out of business when I was in high school. This restaurant opened up a few years later." He paused. "Why are you nervous?"

"The robbery, my aunt's injuries … you. This is so weird, Braden."

He nodded in agreement. "When I got up this morning, I didn't expect to end up having dinner with you."

"Me either. I can't get over how old you are."

"Thanks," he said dryly.

"I didn't mean it in a negative way. You've just been frozen in time in my head, and I'm not used to this new, adult you. Look at us, we're drinking alcohol."

"Well, you are. I'm still looking for a waiter."

"You know what I mean."

"It *is* strange," he conceded. "The last time I had a drink with you was at my cousin Mary's wedding. We sneaked champagne into the garage when no one was looking."

"And I hated the taste of it," she said, remembering those tiny bubbles from a long time ago. "I pretended that I liked it, because I wanted to be cool, but I thought it was disgusting."

"So did I," he said.

"You chugged it."

"Because it was disgusting," he replied with a small smile.

This was the old Braden, the one she'd shared secrets with, her best friend. Her heart warmed as she gazed back at him. "I thought you liked it."

"I wanted to be cool, too."

"Did you learn to like it?"

"Never. What about you?"

She shook her head. "On my 21st birthday, my date bought me a really expensive bottle of champagne, and I didn't have the heart to tell him I didn't like it."

Braden's gaze darkened at the mention of another guy. At least, she thought that was the reason for the sudden shadows in eyes. She didn't have a chance to ask. The waiter appeared to take their drink orders and announce the specials.

Braden ordered a beer, and the waiter said he'd be back in a moment to take the rest of their order.

She picked up her menu, perusing the large selection of entrees. "What's good here?"

"Enchiladas, super burritos, tamales. I haven't had anything bad yet," he replied, as he flipped through the menu.

"Do you eat here a lot?" she asked.

"Since I moved back, I've been here a few

times."

"When did you return?"

"About two months ago."

The waiter returned with Braden's beer and asked if they'd decided.

"I'll have the chicken enchiladas," she said.

"Beef burrito," Braden said, handing over their menus.

After the waiter left, Braden raised his bottle of beer. "Cheers."

She clinked her glass to his bottle and said, "Cheers."

Feeling emboldened by the tequila, she asked, "So do I look different to you, Braden?"

"You're definitely not twelve anymore."

His gaze dropped to her breasts, and she self-consciously crossed her arms. She'd definitely developed some curves since she'd left Sand Harbor.

"You're beautiful, Alexa," he added, his tone husky as he raised his eyes to hers.

Heat ran through her body, warming her cheeks. "You don't have to say that."

"I know I don't have to, but it's true. I always knew you would be."

"I don't see how you could have known that. I had so many freckles when I was a kid, and my hair always frizzed in the salt air. I was too skinny. That stupid friend of yours, Paul, used to say I had horse legs."

"If it makes you feel any better, Paul lost all his hair by the time he was twenty-three."

"Well, good," she said. "I don't feel at all sorry for him."

"I didn't think you would." He paused, taking another swig of beer, his gaze growing more reflective. "You were cute at twelve, but even prettier at sixteen."

She stared at him in surprise. "How would you know that? You didn't see me at sixteen."

"I did see you," he replied. "But you didn't see me."

"What are you talking about? Where were you? Where was I?"

"It was at your high school in Virginia."

"You did not come to Virginia," she denied.

"It was the summer after my father died. There was a school trip to D.C. When the group went to tour the Pentagon, I took a bus to Alexandria. I waited in front of your school until the bell rang. I wasn't sure what I was going to say when I saw you – *if* I saw you. I was just about to give up when you came out with someone -- some guy." His voice turned cold. "He had his arm around you, and he said something, and you laughed. Then he kissed you." Braden shrugged. "So I left." He raised his beer to his lips again.

"Why didn't you say something?" she asked, amazed that he'd come to see her and she'd never known.

"You were with someone else."

"Well, why didn't you tell me you were coming? We could have set something up."

"I wasn't sure I was going to come until the last second," he replied.

She shook her head. "I don't understand, Braden. You told me earlier that you didn't call me back after your dad died because we weren't friends anymore."

"We weren't friends, Alexa. You didn't call or keep in touch. You moved on. So I tried to do the same. But when the trip came up, I thought what the hell, might as well check in. See if there's any reason to talk again."

"I wish you would have said something." Her stomach twisted into a knot of regret at the lost opportunity. "I know I broke my promise to you to keep in touch."

"We don't have to go over this again."

"We do, because you don't understand. My mother was a mess after the divorce. She cried all day and all night. Sometimes, she'd sit in her room and put her arms around her knees, and curl up into this tight, sad little ball, and she'd just rock back and forth and sob like her heart was literally breaking. And when she wasn't crying, she was furious. She moved me back east so that my father couldn't see me. She used me like a weapon, and I couldn't even blame her, because my father was so mean to her. I was the only one she had to lean on, and holding her up took every last bit of strength I had."

Now that she'd started to explain, she couldn't seem to stop. "I felt like I was drowning in her depression, Braden. And I had no one to turn to. All my friends were gone, and you seemed like a million miles away. I knew my mom was never going to let me go back to Sand Harbor, because she and my aunt stopped talking to each other. So every time you asked me when I was coming back, I was lying to you, pretending that it was going to happen. And it just got too hard. I felt … hopeless." She drew in a ragged breath. "It was a bad time in my life."

He frowned. "I had no idea it was that rough. You should have said something."

"I kept thinking I'd wait until I had good news, but good news never came, and then the silence had gone on too long, and I thought you'd probably forgotten about me. When your dad died, I wanted to talk to you so much, but when you didn't call me back, I realized you really were done." Which brought her back to the same surprise she'd felt a moment earlier. "I can't believe you came to see me the next year."

"I didn't forget about you, Alexa. I tried, but I couldn't."

"I didn't forget about you, either. That's why I came here after college." She paused. "We have really bad timing."

"Yeah, we do." He paused. "I wish I'd know how bad your mom was."

"No one knew. She swore me to secrecy, afraid I'd tell you, and you'd tell your mom, who'd tell my aunt... She didn't want my dad to know how much he'd hurt her, at least, most of the time. When she was trying to make a point or asking for more child support, then sometimes she'd let him in on her pain."

"I guess that makes sense," he said slowly.

"Nothing in divorce makes sense."

"Well, that's true."

His response reminded her that he'd had his own share of problems. She sat back in her chair, studying him for a moment. "What happened with your marriage?"

He shook his head, a steel glint in his eyes. "My marriage is not up for discussion, Alexa."

She didn't like his abrupt answer, but Braden had always been private, even as a kid.

"What about you?" he asked.

"I'm not married, if that's the question."

"Significant other?"

"No."

"That's hard to believe."

"I've been busy making a career."

"As an accountant?"

She frowned. "Don't say it like it's a dirty word."

"I just don't get it." He rested his arms on the

table as he leaned forward. "You had such big dreams when you were a kid – the biggest dreams I'd ever heard."

The reminder brought a wave of sadness. She felt as if her life could be divided into parts -- the time before the divorce, and the time after.

"When my family fell apart, my dreams went away, too," she said. "There just didn't seem to be any point. I had to grow up, so I did. You should understand. You were the man of your family long before your dad died. You used to take care of your mom and your brother and sister. You were responsible, realistic, and I was just a silly dreamer."

"I wouldn't say you were silly."

"Well, thanks for that. Is your family still living here?"

"My mother and sister are. My brother is in Portland. He's in law school."

"Law school? In my mind Matt is still five years old."

"Twenty-two now."

"Well, your mom and sister must be happy to have you back."

"They are."

Their conversation was interrupted by the arrival of their food.

"This looks good," she said, picking up her fork. The delicious smell made her stomach rumble, and she realized how long it had been since she'd last eaten.

They ate in silence. As usual, Braden inhaled his food, cleaning his plate before she was halfway through her enchiladas. She smiled. "You were always fast," she said.

"Got faster when I was in the service. I never knew how long I had to eat."

"Where did you serve?"

"I was in Iraq and also in Afghanistan and a bunch of other places you've never heard of."

"How did you get injured?"

"I don't want to talk about it."

"You have a lot of things you don't want to talk about."

"Yes, I do," he said bluntly.

She set down her fork. "Fine. So let's talk about the robbery. I assume Drew didn't give you any new information."

"No. He's been looking into a link between the shipment from the Wellbourne estate and the break-in, but he hasn't found any ties. Wellbourne's sons seem to have no argument with the items being sent to your aunt. They indicated that their father was quite fond of Phoebe."

"Really? That's interesting."

"The lawyer said no one else has come forward to contest anything in the will. Drew thinks it's a dead end."

The spark in his eyes told her he didn't agree with his friend. "But you don't?"

"The only thing that was different about yesterday was that delivery. It could have been the trigger or just a coincidence, but I'm not ready to rule it out."

"What about the wife? Wasn't Jack Wellbourne married at some point?"

"He was married twice, once to the mother of his sons. She died a long time ago. He divorced his second wife, Roberta about six years ago. Drew spoke to Roberta as well, and she doesn't seem to have a problem with anything."

"So everyone is happy."

"That's what they say."

She thought about the castle-like house on the bluff. "I loved the Wellbourne's house on the beach. Remember all the stories we made up? Remember Ariel -- the beautiful woman with the long red hair? I thought she looked like a mermaid or some ghostly bride. We used to see her standing on the balcony wearing that floaty white dress." Alexa could see her so clearly. "Was she a Wellbourne?"

"No, but it's interesting you brought her up," he said slowly, a thoughtful expression entering his eyes.

"Why is it interesting?"

"I haven't thought about her in a very long time, but she died at the end of that summer. Her body washed up on the beach near the pier."

"She drowned?" Alexa echoed in surprise. "That's so sad. She was young. What happened?"

"No one seemed to know. The press descended on the town. It was news, because she was an actress. Rumors were flying for weeks, but it was ruled an accidental death." He sat back in his seat, a contemplative expression on his face.

"What are you thinking?" she asked.

"I'm not sure."

"She was such a mysterious figure," Alexa continued. "She was always on the widow's walk or the deck, looking out to sea, as if she were searching for something or waiting for someone. I used to imagine she was waiting for her lover to come to her." Goosebumps ran down her arms, and she shivered. "But she died a long time ago. Her death couldn't have anything to do with what's happening now."

"She was connected to that house," Braden said. "And she was fighting with someone that last night we were on the beach."

"You're right." The argument they'd overheard had seemed very much like the constant battles being fought by her parents, and it had made her feel a little sick to her stomach. "I wonder who she was fighting with."

"I have no idea. I didn't see anyone. Did you?"

"No. I just remember her yelling something about secrets, and there wasn't just anger in her voice, but pain. She seemed like she had been betrayed."

"I think you're starting to embellish," Braden said with a small smile.

"Maybe. Did you tell anyone about that fight after she died?"

"No. I didn't think about it. I was back in school, and I wasn't paying attention to the news. I'm sure my mom didn't let me go near the beach when the investigation was going on."

"We need to find out more about Ariel."

"I don't think that will be difficult, but as you said, it's doubtful her death is connected to the robbery at your aunt's store."

"But you're as curious as I am," she said, seeing a new light in his eyes.

"I'm a little interested," he conceded. "But I've also been bored out of my mind the last few weeks so that's not saying much."

"The transition from soldier to citizen hasn't been easy for you, I take it."

"Not in any way."

"Do you have any idea what you're going to do next?"

"Well, the next thing I'm going to do is pay the check."

She made a face at him. "You know that's not what I meant."

"It's as far ahead as I'm looking right now." He

pulled out his wallet as the waiter set down their bill. "This is on me."

"We can split it," she offered.

"It's fine. I've got it." He set two twenties down and closed the folder. "You're not going back to the shop tonight, are you?"

She'd thought about it, but she would feel too vulnerable being there alone at night. "I'll leave it for tomorrow. I'm exhausted," she said as she got to her feet.

"That's a good idea. I don't think you should be alone there at night anyway."

"You think the thief might come back?" A chill ran down her spine at the thought. Had someone been watching her all day? Waiting for her to leave?

"It's possible. Why don't you go back to the Inn and get some rest? Drew will have patrols going past the shop all night. There's nothing more for you to do at the moment."

"That's a good idea. I think it would feel a little too creepy at night."

They walked out to the front of the restaurant, pausing on the sidewalk.

"I'll see you to your hotel," he said.

"It's practically next door," she said. "I can make it."

"All right."

"Braden," she said as he started to leave. "I really wish you'd said something when you came to see me in Virginia."

"There was no point," he said.

"You don't know that. Maybe if we'd reconnected then…" She couldn't finish the thought because she didn't know what would have happened.

He shook his head. "It doesn't matter now. We're different people. I'm not the same kid you once knew."

"I think he's still in there somewhere."

His expression only turned grim. "No, he's long gone, Alexa. Don't go looking for him. You'll only be disappointed."

Chapter Four

Alexa was still thinking about Braden's words when she returned to the Cheshire Inn. There had been anger and pain in his voice when he'd talked about how he'd changed, as if he'd disappointed himself. That was surprising. Evie had made it sound like Braden had come out of the service as a hero, but he certainly wasn't acting that way. She wished she knew what he'd gone through, but he obviously wasn't interested in telling her. He wanted her to leave it alone, and that would certainly be the smart thing to do, but she'd never been very good at shutting down her curiosity. And when it came to Braden she was intensely curious.

Braden had been important to her from the first minute she'd met him. He'd filled up all the lonely spaces in her soul. He'd become her whole world, the one person she could really talk to, the only person who would really listen. There had been a depth to their friendship that had gone far beyond a sweet, little love between two budding teenagers. Their home lives had been fraught with uncertainty. Alone, they'd felt vulnerable; together they'd been invincible.

But their time had passed. They couldn't go back to what they were. They couldn't recreate what they'd had as kids. Once loved died, it was dead. There was no resurrecting it. And who even wanted to try to bring love back? When it ended, it usually turned to hate. She'd seen that happen with her parents. Two people who had vowed to love each other until death turned into people who actually wanted to kill each other. She couldn't live with that kind of extreme emotion. It was too much. So she did everything she could to avoid any relationship that would take her into that tense, unsettling space. It hadn't been that difficult to find guys who just wanted to have a good time. In fact, she was probably the ideal date for most men.

But a relationship with Braden would be different. They'd already been too close. They could never pull off emotional distance now. Maybe if he had said something to her when he'd come to see her in high school. Perhaps then it wouldn't have been too late. Still, she couldn't quite imagine how that scenario would have played out. She'd been on the other side of the country. They would have had to do long distance, and they'd already proved they weren't good at that – at least she wasn't.

It was futile to think of what might have been. They were different people now. Braden was right about that. They'd both changed. Who knew if they would even like each other if they spent a few days together? Maybe they would drive each other crazy. It could be a good test.

No, she shook off that tempting thought. It would be too risky to get involved with him. She'd already loved him and lost him. She didn't want to go through that hurt again. It would be far better for her to get out of town as soon as possible and go back to her real life.

With a sigh, she told herself to stop thinking about Braden and focus on the task at hand. She'd come to Sand Harbor to help her aunt, and while she couldn't do anything to help Phoebe recover physically, she could try to find out who had broken into the store. The only link she had was the

Wellbournes, and the police had already started looking into that family. But what about Ariel -- the woman who had spent time at the Wellbourne's beach house and had died so tragically? Who was she? Did she have a connection to the family? Or was she just a random renter?

Sitting down on her bed, Alexa opened her laptop computer and started a search for a female drowning in Sand Harbor fifteen years ago. It didn't take long to get an answer or a picture. The first photo appeared to be a professional headshot. The stunning redhead with light green eyes, full, sexy lips and flawless skin was Shayla Cummings, a twenty-five-year-old model turned actress.

According to the accompanying article, two local surfers had discovered Shayla's lifeless body on the beach in the early morning hours. The coroner's report stated she'd been in the water for more than thirty-six hours. The cause of death was drowning. There was no evidence of foul play.

Alexa frowned at the bare details. She needed more information. She flipped through the search results again and found more details about Shayla's life. She'd been born Sharon Cummings but had changed her name to Shayla when she started modeling. She was the child of a broken home. Her father took off when she was a kid, and her mother got her into commercials as a baby, using Shayla to make money to support the family.

As a teenager, Shayla made a name for herself as a swimsuit model for *Sports Illustrated*. In her late teens, early twenties, she had a string of relationships with sports stars and celebrities, including a few married men. Her relationship with director, Craig Bellamy, had landed her the lead role in a big blockbuster film. Unfortunately, the movie was a blockbuster failure and Shayla's performance was harshly reviewed in the press. Most Hollywood insiders doubted she'd ever work as an actress again.

Shayla's sister, Dana, said that Shayla had gone to Sand Harbor to get away from the paparazzi and to find some peace in her life. It had been a whirlwind two years, and she needed to regroup. She'd chosen Sand Harbor because the town held special memories. Their father used to take them there for summers before he divorced their mother.

A chill ran down Alexa's spine. There were eerie parallels between Shayla's childhood and her own, at least the part about the broken home, and the summers in Sand Harbor.

Alexa skimmed the rest of the article, pausing on the final paragraph, which suggested that some of Shayla's friends thought that her death might not have been an accident but a suicide. One friend even speculated that it could have been murder based on the fact that Shayla was wearing a long, white dress when she was found. Who goes swimming all dressed up?

Alexa caught her breath, thinking about that beautiful dress that she'd so admired. Shayla had always seemed like a romantic and tragic figure on the deck of that big, mysterious house. Had she killed herself? Or had someone killed her?

Alexa felt cold at the thought and told herself to get a grip. Obviously, the police had looked into the incident at the time.

She continued searching but soon discovered that there wasn't much more to be learned about Shayla's death. While there were numerous photos pairing Shayla with handsome, rich men, there was nothing that tied her to any of the Wellbournes. There was also a distinct lack of information in the local papers.

Why was that? There wasn't much in the way of hard news in Sand Harbor, so why hadn't someone dug into Shayla's death in greater detail?

Alexa couldn't find an interview with anyone in town, with the exception of the one brief, quoted statement from the police department regarding the coroner's report. The local paper would give three long columns to the annual pumpkin festival but not cover an unexplained death on the shore? That didn't make sense.

Flopping back against the pillows, Alexa stared up at the ceiling. The fact that she'd seen Shayla arguing with someone just a few days before her death seemed important. Was that person tied up in Shayla's death? Had she and Braden witnessed something important but just hadn't known it at the time?

She glanced at her cell phone on the bedside table, wishing she could call Braden, but he hadn't given her his number. She needed to talk to someone, if only to get out of her own head awhile and take a break from her imagination. She thought about contacting one of her friends at home, but San Francisco felt very far away.

After a small hesitation, she picked up the phone and called Evie. She might as well check in with the family.

"You must have ESP," Evie said. "I was just picking up the phone to call you when I saw your name flash on my screen."

"Is there any news on Aunt Phoebe?"

"Yes, good news," Evie said, excitement in her voice. "Aunt Phoebe woke up this evening. She was dazed and disoriented and drifted back to sleep fairly quickly, but the doctor said it's a good sign, and he's optimistic about her making a full recovery."

"Thank God," she said, feeling an enormous wave of relief. "That is the best news."

"I feel like a weight just fell off my shoulders," Evie said. "I sent her friends home, but I suspect they'll be back first thing in the morning. They're very dedicated."

"She's lucky to have so many people who care about her. I'll go see her in the morning."

"She would love that. I told her that you were taking care of the store, and she was very pleased."

"Did she say anything about what happened last night? Do you think she can identify the thief or thieves?"

"I didn't ask her about the assault. The doctor said not to stress her out, to take things slow. I did speak to Drew Lassen at the police department and told him that he should be able to interview her tomorrow."

"Well, that's good. Maybe she'll be able to give us enough information to find whoever put her in the hospital."

"I hope so. The hospital placed a security guard outside her room for tonight."

Alexa's heart jumped with alarm. "Is she in danger?"

"They don't want to take any chances, and I feel better knowing that someone is watching over her."

"Me, too."

"How did things go at the store today?" Evie asked.

"I wish I could say I made a lot of progress, but I still have more boxes to go through. I'll tackle those tomorrow."

"Aunt Phoebe will appreciate whatever you do. I wish I could help, but I have my hands full with the kids tomorrow. We have a field trip, and I'm a chaperone, so I'll be gone all day. I might be able to get in some time on Saturday. And Aunt Phoebe's assistant should be back next week."

"It's not a problem. I like having something productive to do."

"You loved working there as a kid. I always thought it was a little boring, all that old stuff," Evie confessed.

"But there's so much history attached to each piece. It's fun to think about all the people who used the furniture. It's like a window into time."

"You sound like Aunt Phoebe now."

Alexa smiled to herself. It was nice to feel connected to her aunt. She'd really missed this side of the family.

"Aunt Phoebe said you could stay at her house," Evie added. "The spare key is still on the shelf in the garden shed if you feel like making a move."

"I'm very comfortable here. But if you need me to take care of anything at the house, I can do that, too."

"I already went by and fed her cat, so we're good for tonight. I feel badly that I've left you on your own though. Did you get some dinner?"

"I did. I went to La Cantina."

"They have great food. I hope you didn't feel uncomfortable eating on your own."

Alexa hesitated, knowing that whatever she said was going to generate some questions, but it wasn't a secret, and not talking about it would make it more important than it was. "I wasn't on my own," she said. "Braden stopped by the shop, and we talked for a bit, and then we went to dinner."

Evie let out a squeal of surprise. "Are you serious? You already ran into Braden? I thought you weren't going to see him."

"It wasn't my idea. Drew Lassen asked him to help with the investigation. I guess they're shorthanded with some politician in town and others out with the flu or on vacation. Braden isn't a cop, but apparently he has some experience in military intelligence, although he didn't want to talk about it."

"Did he tell you about his divorce?"

"He didn't want to talk about that either. He was very closed off."

"That's not surprising. I'm actually shocked he went out with you at all. He's been holed up in a dumpy apartment on South Street for weeks. I play Bunco with his sister, Carey, and she said she's really worried about him, that he's not the same, that he's in some dark place now."

"Well, it's been a long time since I saw him, so it's difficult for me to judge whether he's changed since he went to war or if he's different because it has been fifteen years since we hung out together. I would agree, however, that he seems a little dark. I'm sure he needs time to work things through."

"Maybe it's good for him to reconnect with you. Perhaps you'll remind him of who he used to be. Hold on a sec," Evie added.

Alexa could hear her cousin yelling to her kid to brush his teeth. Then Evie came back on the line.

"I have to run. It's story time here. I'll talk to you tomorrow."

"Sure. Good-night," Alexa said.

She ended the call, set her phone on the bed, then glanced back at the computer. Instead of searching for Shayla again, she typed in Braden's name. She wondered if there was any information about what he'd gone through on the other side of the world. Ten minutes later, she shut off the computer with a frustrated sigh. If she was going to find out what had happened to Braden, he would have to tell her. She doubted that would happen any time soon, and with her aunt on the way to recovery, how long would she even be in town? The police were investigating. She could leave them to it.

But she knew if she walked away now, she'd regret it.

For fifteen years she'd been haunted by Braden and her very first kiss. She'd always felt like their relationship had been ripped away, that they had unfinished business. It was time to finish it. She needed closure, and she wasn't going to get that if she left now.

* * *

Braden dragged his old bike down the stairs of his apartment building early Thursday morning. It was one of the few items he'd retrieved from the house he'd shared with his soon-to-be ex-wife on the other side of town. He'd always loved to ride, but it had been a long time since he'd been on his bike, probably since before he'd enlisted.

When he reached the parking lot behind his building, he hopped on, hoping the tires would make it to the nearest gas station where he could put in some air. His right thigh protested as he started to pedal, the muscles still painful from the recent tear in his quad muscle. But it felt good to ride, the wind in his face, the sun on his head, the smell of salt water in the air. It was springtime in Sand Harbor, a new beginning for nature and maybe for him, too.

The last few months had been brutal. He hadn't handled his injuries, his marriage, or his discharge from the Army at all well. It had been too much to deal with at one time. But he was tired of feeling out of it, of sitting in his apartment all day long, drifting aimlessly... He'd always been active. He'd always had goals.

Unfortunately, all of his early goals had been about following in his dad's very impressive footsteps. Now, he didn't know what he wanted to do.

As he rode toward the downtown area, he couldn't help thinking about Alexa. Bike riding had been their thing. From June to August, he'd gotten up every morning and met Alexa on the corner by her aunt's house. They'd taken off together each day on a new adventure. Even when they didn't do more than just ride around, their days were full, fun. They connected on so many levels. They didn't even have to talk to understand each other.

At first, it had just been a friendship. They'd met when they were ten, but by the time they were twelve, he'd definitely started noticing how pretty she was, how much he wanted to put his arm around her, hold her hand, maybe even kiss her. He'd finally gotten his courage up that last day, that last moment.

One kiss, that's all they'd had.

He'd kissed a lot of other girls since then. He'd even married one. But Alexa had never completely left his mind. She'd always been there, somewhere in the background, an unrealized dream.

His friends from school had been happy when Alexa stopped coming around. When she was in town, he'd ditched them to spend time with her. He couldn't help himself. Her beautiful smile had literally lit up his world. And then she was gone. It wasn't her fault. She'd been a kid, and her parents had made her leave, but he'd never imagined that that last day on the beach would be the last day he'd see her for many, many years. He'd never considered that she wouldn't write, wouldn't call him every other second.

For years, he'd thought they'd meet up again, but when he had finally gone to see her in high school, she'd been with someone else. It hadn't really surprised him. Why wouldn't she have moved on from the childhood crush they'd had on each other? It had been years.

He was a little surprised that Alexa had come back to Sand Harbor after college. He couldn't believe it was to see him, although part of him wanted to think that way. But it had probably been more of a desire to reconnect with her aunt and maybe check in on him at the same time. He'd been married by then. Married and in the Army. He'd rushed into both.

But all that was in the past. Alexa was here now. He was here, too. For the first time in a long time they were in the same physical space. But mentally, they were no doubt miles apart.

He was still reeling from the events of the past few months, and he had way too much emotional baggage to even think of dumping it on someone else. Alexa would press him to talk. She'd already started asking questions, and he knew that wasn't going to stop any time soon, but he didn't want to tell her about his past. Not just because he didn't want to share the horrific details, but also because he didn't really want her to look at him differently. And she would.

Kinley had.

The thought of his soon-to-be ex-wife made him pedal harder – faster.

Kinley had been a huge mistake. They'd met three months before they married. It had been fast and fun and completely foolish. They'd been twenty years old, old enough to know better, but young enough to still be stupid. Kinley hadn't known what she was getting herself into, and he hadn't either. He'd believed they'd be like his parents, who had married young and been incredibly happy. When he'd thought of the Army, he'd seen in his head the picture of his father in his uniform, the photo that had sat on the mantel in his mother's living room for his entire life. That picture had shown a man who was perfect and proud, one objective in his eyes, to serve his country and protect his family, not a hint of doubt about his career choice. The war Braden had gotten himself into had had very few clear objectives. It had been chaotic and bloody, one win turning into two losses, a never-ending fight that he doubted could ever be won. His marriage had turned out to be just as messy.

It was over now – all of it. He needed to move on.

He stopped at the gas station and filled up his tires, and then headed toward the harbor. It was only a few miles and mostly flat, so not a difficult ride. It was a beautiful day, with only a few white clouds to mar the vast blue sky. When he'd been overseas, he'd carried this picture in his head: the picturesque downtown streets with the open air cafés and boutiques, the boats gently swaying in the harbor, and the fishermen selling the day's catch every afternoon. Sand Harbor was what the world should be, he thought -- peaceful, calm, pretty. But the rest of the world wasn't like that at all, at least not the places he'd traveled the past few years.

When he reached the antique store, he felt a surge of anticipation. He parked his bike by the tree in front of the store and was just about to knock when Alexa opened the door.

"Hi," she said, her smile a bit tentative. "I saw you through the window."

"I figured you'd be in here early. You always liked a treasure hunt."

"I wish we were just looking for treasure." She stepped back and waved him inside, locking the door behind him.

"Any news on your aunt?"

"Yes, she woke up last night, and the doctor thinks she's going to make a full recovery. I stopped in early this morning, but she was still asleep. I'm going to go back later."

"I'm glad," he said, seeing the relief in her eyes.

"Me, too. So after I left you last night, I did a little research on Ariel, otherwise known as Shayla Cummings."

"What did you find out?"

"That Shayla was a model turned actress, whose first movie bombed, but she was comforted by quite a lineup of attractive men and power players. Unfortunately, I couldn't tie any of those men to Sand Harbor," Alexa added. "And what also disturbs me is that the local news coverage was so skimpy in regards to her death. This town never has anything newsworthy to report, yet the drowning of a beautiful actress only gets a couple of paragraphs? I don't get it."

"I noticed that, too."

She gave him a knowing smile. "So I wasn't the only one who was curious."

"I couldn't stop thinking about that fight we witnessed," he admitted.

"Exactly. What if we saw something, and we didn't realize it at the time," she said, an excited note in her voice. "We didn't know she was going to die a short while later, so we weren't paying attention in any particular way. But we were the only ones on the beach that night. We could have been the only witnesses."

"But we don't know what we witnessed," he said, trying to dampen her enthusiasm. He could feel himself getting caught up in her story the way he always had. He tried to tell himself to keep it real, get a grip, but then he thought what the hell – it had been months since he'd been interested in anything. Pondering a fifteen-year-old mystery wasn't the worst thing he could be thinking about. "I do have a theory on the lack of newspaper coverage. Jack Wellbourne owned the building where the newspaper was housed back then."

"You think he had some influence over the newspaper coverage?"

Braden shrugged. "It's possible. He was their landlord, and he owned a lot of buildings in town. It might have been difficult for them to move or to ignore him."

"It always comes back to the Wellbournes," she mused. "Shayla was living in their house, the newspaper was owned by Jack Wellbourne, and these boxes came from the Wellbourne estate."

"Three for three," he muttered.

"Exactly."

"But it's not a good idea to get so focused on one possibility that we overlook everything else," he warned. "We need to keep an open mind."

"So what do we do next? I've looked through all the boxes. I still need to do a detailed inventory, but nothing jumped out at me. I also don't know what I'm looking for, something valuable, something sentimental, something damaging?" She gave a helpless shrug. "Or maybe whatever the thief wanted, they already got. Who knows?"

"Well, if the boxes haven't provided any clues, maybe we should look at where they came from."

"The house on the beach?"

"Exactly."

"Isn't it empty? And isn't it also probably locked?"

"Only one way to find out," he replied.

"It could be a wild goose chase, Braden."

"Your favorite kind as I recall."

She smiled. "True. However, the practical thing to do would be to stay here and take inventory."

"When did you get so practical?"

"The day I left here -- fifteen years ago."

He could see her wrestle with the tug from the past, the same tug he felt. "The boxes aren't going anywhere," he said.

"Do you really want to go back to the beach?" she asked.

He could tell by the look in her eyes that her question had more to do with their past than Shayla's. Maybe it was a mistake, but God help him, he did want to see her on the beach again.

"Okay," she said suddenly, obviously deciding not to wait for his answer. "We'll go to the beach. But first I want to stop by the hospital."

"Sounds good. I'd like to see your aunt, too."

"Maybe she'll be able to tell us who assaulted her and then this will also be over," Alexa added.

"Maybe," he said, feeling a little guilty for not wanting it to be over just yet. He wanted to spend more time with Alexa before she went back to her real life, and before he went back to his life -- whatever that was going to be.

Chapter Five

Braden stashed his bike inside the store, and then Alexa drove them both to the hospital. She was acutely conscious of his presence in her compact rental car. She still hadn't quite reconciled the man he was now with the boy she remembered. And Braden wasn't opening up that much. While he was chatty enough about the Wellbournes and Shayla, most of his personal life appeared to be off limits.

She was dying to find out more about the woman he'd married. What had driven him to marry so young? Was he simply following in his father's footsteps again? His father had asked his mother to marry him after their high school graduation. They'd waited a year to tie the knot, but they still hadn't been out of their teens when they'd said *I do*. As a child, she'd thought his parents had the most romantic love story. But sadly their story had ended in tragedy.

Cynically, she wondered if anyone ever lived happily ever after. She certainly hadn't had much experience with long married couples.

Her aunt had supposedly been happy in her marriage, but her husband had also died young. He'd been a fisherman, and he hadn't made it back from a deadly storm. Her aunt had been single ever since, saying she'd already had the love of her life.

As her thoughts turned to her aunt, she said a silent prayer for a quick recovery. Phoebe was a strong woman, and she was going to need that strength now to recover fully from her injuries and the trauma she must have suffered when she realized her store was being robbed.

"Are you thinking about your aunt?" Braden asked.

She gave him a quick look. "You read my mind."

"I've had some practice," he said lightly.

She nodded. There had been a time when they could both read each other's minds, but Braden's thoughts were locked behind a guard wall. Hers apparently were not so difficult to see. "I just want her to be okay," she said.

"It sounds like she will be."

"I'll feel better when I see her."

She turned into the hospital lot and parked the car. Upon arrival, they discovered that Phoebe had been moved out of Intensive Care and into a private room on the third floor. As they exited the elevator, they saw a crowd of people spilling out of the nearby waiting room.

"Looks like half the town is here," Braden observed.

Their arrival drew more than a few surprised looks and subsequent murmurs. Alexa wondered if they were shocked she was in town or that she was with Braden. He seemed to be generating some interest, too.

"Keep walking," he said on a hushed note, hustling her past the waiting room and down the hall.

"You're not being very friendly," she said.

"Trust me, if we start talking to those people, we'll never get out." When they reached her aunt's room, he said, "I'll wait out here for you."

She glanced down the hall, seeing a couple of women looking in their direction. "You'll be a target."

"I can take it," he said shortly, although he didn't

look at all happy about the idea.

"Why don't you come in with me? I'm sure Aunt Phoebe would love to see you, too."

"All right. If you don't mind, I think I will."

She knocked on the partially open door and then pushed it open. She was immediately reassured to see her aunt's eyes open. A nurse was standing by the head of the bed.

"Shall I come back?" she asked.

"No, please come in, Alexa," her aunt said, lifting a weak hand to wave her forward.

"Don't stay too long," the nurse said, as she moved across the room. "She needs to rest."

Her aunt offered her a tired smile. "Alexa, it's so good to see you."

"It's even better to see you awake." Her aunt's skin was pale, and her thinning blonde hair seemed more gray than platinum. There was dark bruising around her eyes and nose and a bandage around her head. She looked very small in the bed and not at all like the bustling, energetic woman she was.

Phoebe's eyes widened as her gaze moved past Alexa. "Braden? Is that you? You're here with Alexa? I can hardly believe it."

"I'm glad you're feeling better," he said, joining Alexa at the bed.

"My goodness, it's been a long time since I saw the two of you together. You were just kids then."

"We were," Braden said.

"How are you feeling, Aunt Phoebe?" Alexa interrupted, knowing that neither she nor Braden wanted to talk about why they were together.

"I have a bad headache," Phoebe said with a wince. "But I'll survive. I'm a tough old broad."

Alexa smiled. Her aunt had always had a strong will. There was no doubt about that. "Did they tell you when you might be able to go home?" she asked.

"The doctor thinks I should stay a couple of days," Phoebe said with annoyance. "I don't know why. I can sleep at home same as I can sleep here."

"Well, you need to do what the doctor says."

"He's young," Phoebe said. "How much could he know?"

"More than you, Aunt Phoebe. You need to listen to him. I'm taking care of the shop for you, so you don't have to worry about that."

"Evie told me you were unpacking for me. You don't have to do that, Alexa."

"I want to. Every new piece is a discovery. It's fun."

Her aunt let out a weary sigh. "You sound just like me."

As her aunt's voice drifted away, Alexa debated her options. She wanted to ask some questions, but despite her aunt's confident attitude, she still didn't look well. Then again, they needed some answers, and waiting might only make things worse. "Aunt Phoebe, do you remember what happened when you went to the antique store night before last?"

"I don't," she said with a sigh. "Everyone keeps asking, and I try to remember, but it's all shadows in my mind."

"What do you remember?" Braden asked. "Start with how you got there. Did you drive?"

"I did drive. I parked in back like I always do," she said.

"So you went in the back door?" Braden continued.

Her aunt nodded. "Yes."

"What happened next?" Braden asked.

Alexa watched as her aunt's brows knit together. She liked the way Braden was taking it slow, one step at a time. And he was so calm, so patient. She could see that his approach was helping her aunt to relax.

"I put my purse down on the desk in the back room." Her gaze narrowed. "Oh, dear, I bet it's still there."

"I'll look for it when I go back and I'll bring it to you," Alexa said.

"Thank you. There's no cash, but I do have my credit cards in it."

"After you set your purse down, what did you do?" Braden asked, bringing Phoebe back to the subject at hand.

"I grabbed the first box by the back door and took it into the office."

"Why did you do that?" Alexa asked. "Why not just unpack in the storeroom?"

"It was in my way. I couldn't even get into the showroom. So I thought I'd put some of the smaller boxes in the office. I was going to make a nice, orderly stack. I do love things organized. It's so much easier to find everything. Whenever I get a delivery, I have to unpack it right away. It just bothers me so much to have boxes sitting around."

"Then what?" Braden asked, obviously sensing that her aunt was getting off track.

"I heard a noise," Phoebe said, looking a little surprised. "I just remembered that. Something broke. It sounded like glass. I stepped into the showroom and I was about to turn on the lights when something bright flashed in my eye. I think I saw the shadow of someone. Maybe he had a flashlight."

Alexa caught her breath, watching her aunt wrestle with her memory.

Phoebe's frown grew deeper. "I don't know what happened next. I feel like I might have screamed, but I don't know if that was just in my head." She paused.

"Then I woke up here in the hospital. I guess I hit my head on the counter or something." Her aunt's voice rose. "Or did someone hit me? Who would do that?"

"You don't need to think about that," Alexa said quickly. As much as she wanted information, she didn't want her aunt to stress herself out, and it was clear she was becoming agitated. "We don't need to talk about this anymore."

Her words did little to reassure her aunt. "I've just never had anything like this happen before," Phoebe said. "And I don't know what was stolen. My assistant won't be back until Monday, so it's frustrating not knowing what I've lost."

"I know you didn't have a chance to look through the boxes that you received from the Wellbourne estate," Braden said, "but did you have any idea what he was sending you? Do you think there were some valuable items included?"

"Everything I sell in my store has value," Phoebe replied. "But if you're asking if there was some big, expensive piece of jewelry or something, I don't know. Jack was a wealthy man, and he had a lot of interesting pieces that he picked up on his travels. I'm itching to see what he sent me. I hope there's some rare treasure." Shadows dimmed her gaze. "I guess anything valuable is probably gone now."

"I don't know how much the thief got," Alexa said. "A couple of the boxes were intact, so your sudden arrival obviously deterred them."

"I guess it's good I was there then."

"How well did you know Jack Wellbourne?" Alexa asked.

Phoebe smiled. "Jack was very charming and had a big personality. We had dinner a few times in recent years. He was a huge flirt, trying to turn my head with flattery, but I could see right through him. I told him to stop wasting his time. Once he backed off a little, I did enjoy his company. We had some things in common. He was a widower, too. His first wife died of breast cancer. It was very sad. Jack wasn't the same after that. He started dating younger women," she said with a touch of disapproval in her voice. "That second wife of his was a real piece of work. Roberta had her eye on the prize though. She saw in Jack the opportunity to gain money and power, and she went after him. He told me later, he got involved with her, because he knew he'd never break her heart. She didn't want love. She just wanted money. I think they both cheated on each other. There were always rumors flying around about them. Then one day she was gone."

Alexa wondered if Jack had cheated on his second wife with Shayla. But wouldn't there have been an even bigger age gap? "How old was Jack?" she asked.

"He was sixty-four, five years older than me. That's young these days."

"It is young. How did he die?"

"Cancer. He got the diagnosis last year. He didn't tell me until six weeks ago." She gave a sad sigh. "That disease seems to take so many of my friends. It's terrible."

Alexa nodded in agreement as she mentally calculated that fifteen years ago Jack would have been forty-nine years old and Shayla was twenty-five. That fit with what her aunt had just told her about Jack's predilection for younger women.

"Jack built the house on the beach for his first wife, Laura," Phoebe continued. "It was Laura's fantasy house. She loved to paint out on the deck in the late afternoons. After she died, Jack couldn't bear to live there, so he rented it out most of the year, and he traveled. After his last divorce, he settled in there. I guess he finally decided to come home." She paused. "Why are you asking me so much about the Wellbournes, Alexa?"

"It just seems like a coincidence that the boxes arrive and someone breaks into your shop," she replied.

Phoebe frowned. "I didn't think of it like that."

"We don't know that the two events are connected," Alexa said quickly. "I don't want you to worry. I'm going to stick around and help you figure out what happened and get things put back together in the shop. Once your assistant gets back next week, we can talk about when you'll be able to reopen."

"You can take time off work?"

"Yes, it's no longer the busy tax season. And I'd like to help you."

"Your mother won't like it," Phoebe said, giving her a pointed look.

That was probably true, but Alexa didn't care. "I'm a grown woman now. I do what I want."

"You should stay at my house."

"I have a room at the Cheshire Inn."

"But you're family, honey."

"I'm fine there, really."

"Well, if you need anything, the spare key is where it always was."

"Okay." She paused, seeing a question in her aunt's eyes. "Is there something else?"

"I was just wondering if your father knows I'm in the hospital."

She'd been covering for her dad for too many years, Alexa thought, always having to explain away some bad behavior on his part. But now wasn't the time to get into the truth about her father with her aunt. "I left him a message. I'm sure he'll be in touch."

Phoebe smiled sadly. "I'm not so sure. Rob is not the man I thought he was." She took a breath, licking her dry lips. "You know I had to raise Rob and Stan after our parents died, and I guess I tried to make up for the loss by giving them what I thought they wanted. I probably spoiled Rob. He was the baby of the family. I just wanted him to be happy. But I didn't realize the extent of his selfishness. When Rob and your mom split up, I took his side. I gave him the benefit of the doubt. I should have treated your mother with more kindness. I didn't know all the facts then, and I shouldn't have chosen sides the way I did. I regret that. I lost you because of it."

Alexa was touched by the apology. "You didn't lose me, Aunt Phoebe, I'm right here. Don't think about any of that now. Do you want me to stay for a while and keep you company?"

"No, no, you and Braden have better things to do. I'm fine. I think I have some friends in the waiting room."

"Only most of the town," she said with a smile. "You're very popular. I'll be back later."

"All right, dear. Thank you for coming. And you, too, Braden. It's nice to see you on your feet."

He tipped his head. "It's good to *be* on my feet."

"Your mother was worried about you when you were overseas. She's happy you're back now. We all are. I hope you're going to stay."

"We'll see," he said. "You take care."

"I will. And thank you for helping Alexa. I always felt like she was safe when she was with you. It's good you have an opportunity to reconnect."

Alexa smiled. If her aunt still had the energy to match make, she couldn't be feeling too badly. "Good-bye," she said, leaning over to give her aunt a kiss on the cheek.

After leaving the room, Alexa and Braden walked back down the hall. Louise, one of her aunt's best friends, asked if it was all right to go in, and Alexa nodded. "Just a few at a time," she added.

"Don't worry, we won't overwhelm her," Louise said. "We just want her to feel our support."

"I'm sure she already does."

She moved toward the elevator where Braden was waiting. He had his back to the crowd, his stance making it clear he wasn't interested in conversation.

"It's okay. They're not interested in you at the moment," she said.

He flung a quick glance over his shoulder. A few of her aunt's friends were headed toward her room while the others were resuming their seats in the waiting room.

"Thank God for that," he said with a sigh.

"Aunt Phoebe looked really pale."

"She's going to be all right. She's as tough as she said."

"I'd forgotten how much she always liked you."

"She thought I protected you. Little did she know you were the one with all the bad ideas," Braden said, a small smile on his lips. "The only person I had to protect you from was yourself."

She shook her head. "That is not true."

"Yes, it is."

"You had some bad ideas, too, Braden."

"Like what?"

"I'm thinking," she retorted.

He grinned. "Yeah, you keep thinking, because you're not going to be able to come up with anything."

"I'm sure I will," she said, not really caring that Braden was putting all the blame on her, because for the first time since she'd come back, he sounded like the old Braden. God, she'd missed that boy.

The elevator doors opened, and they got in. She pushed the button for the lobby as Braden said, "I'm surprised your father isn't here."

"I'm not. He can't be counted on to show up anywhere."

"Sounds like your aunt has finally seen him for who he is."

"It was nice of her to recognize that she treated my mother harshly. She just couldn't go against her brother. I understood that, but it still hurt."

"Do you still see your dad, Alexa?"

"I've seen him probably three times in the last seven years. He came to my high school graduation, my college graduation, and I went to the hospital when his fourth child was born. He barely spoke to me. I don't have any relationship with his kids. I always wanted brothers and sisters, and now I have four half-siblings that I don't even see. I have no idea what they think about me."

"How old are they?"

"They're young, elementary school age."

She was relieved when the elevator doors opened. She didn't want to talk about her father and his second family. It was too painful.

"Shall we go to the beach now?" she asked as they headed back to the car.

"Sounds like a good idea."

"Really? I thought I only had bad ideas," she said lightly.

He smiled. "Well, we'll see how this one turns out."

* * *

Alexa parked her car by the harbor. Then she and Braden walked the three blocks to a narrow, pebbly path that led down to the beach. A pair of bikes locked around a wooden fence pole reminded her of all the times they'd put their bikes in the exact same place. It also reminded her of the very last time they'd left this beach, and the one and only time Braden had kissed her.

Braden didn't seem to be taking the same slow trip down memory lane. Instead, he walked briskly ahead of her.

When they hit the sand, she gave a sigh of appreciation as the water came into view. She'd always loved the ocean, the crash of the waves on the beach, the squawking of birds as they dove into the sea in search of food, and the misty salt spray that always seemed to linger on her lips.

Despite the fact that it was a Thursday, more than a few people were getting a head start on the weekend. An older couple strolled hand in hand along the shoreline. A father was throwing a Frisbee to his kids, another young couple was trying to launch a kite, and a lone man was tossing a tennis ball to his dog, who plunged happily in and out of the water.

As they walked across the sand, Alexa found her gaze drifting downward. She'd spent many hours on this beach looking for sea glass, a popular phenomenon on this part of the coast. A pang of regret hit her as she thought about all those beautiful pieces of glass that she'd wanted to turn into something beautiful. She'd left her last collection behind at her aunt's house. She wondered if it was still there.

Her dawdling made the distance between her and Braden greater. She didn't understand his mood.

Gone was the lighthearted man who had teased her about having bad ideas. Since they'd arrived at the beach, he'd gone cold and hard. His entire body was one tight muscle, and he was practically running down the beach. Whatever he was thinking about now was not making him happy. She wondered what had changed.

Breaking into a light jog, she had just about caught up with him when he stopped abruptly, grabbed his leg and fell to the ground.

She ran over to him, dropping to her knees by his side. "What's wrong?"

He grimaced as he clutched his right thigh. "Cramp," he gritted out.

"Can I do something?"

He shook his head, his face a mask of pain. "It will pass."

She hated seeing him suffering, and she had nothing to offer, not even a bottle of water. She reached out a hand, thinking she'd offer to massage the cramping muscle, but he pushed her away.

"Don't," he said shortly.

"Sorry."

She watched and waited. The tension in his face gradually began to ease. Finally, he moved into a sitting position, wincing as he stretched out his leg.

"Is it better?" she asked.

Angry, hurt pride filled his eyes as his gaze met hers. Braden had always hated to look weak. "Yes," he said shortly.

"You know this reminds me of the 4th of July carnival," she said, shifting into a more relaxed position.

"What are you talking about?" he grumbled.

"You pulled your hamstring during the three-legged race, but you wouldn't admit you were in pain.

You insisted on finishing. You were determined to win."

"And we did win," he pointed out.

"Yes, but you couldn't walk for a month after that."

"What's your point?"

"That you're stubborn and you never admit when you're hurting."

"Fine, I admit it. I'm in pain."

She tilted her head, studying him for a moment. She decided it was time to risk asking another big question. "What happened to you, Braden? How were you injured?"

He hesitated for a long moment, then said. "There was an explosion – gunfire – I was shot a couple of times, once in the leg. It ripped through my muscle."

"Were you the only one that was hurt?"

"No. There were several casualties."

Her heart filled with compassion, sensing that he'd lost someone important to him. "One of your friends?"

"Yes. I don't want to talk about him."

"It might help. Just tell me his name."

He drew in a breath and then said, "Pete Connors."

The name rang a distant bell. "You used to hang around with a kid named Pete," she said. "It wasn't the same guy, was it?"

"The very same. We grew up together, enlisted in the army together, did pretty much everything together. But I came back, and Pete didn't." Braden paused, turning his gaze toward the water. "His parents can't even look at me – his wife either. They want to know how come I made it, and he didn't. I ask myself the same question."

"I'm sorry, Braden." She wished she had more to offer than an apology, but any platitudes would only piss him off. His wounds were too deep and too personal.

He shrugged as if he didn't care, but he did. He probably cared too much.

"I'm glad you made it," she said. "If you ever do want to talk about it, I'll listen."

"That won't happen."

"Well, if it does, I'll…"

His gaze narrowed at her pause. "Were you going to say you would be here for me? But you can't say that, can you?"

She had stopped herself, realizing she was about to make a promise she might not be able to keep. "I don't know where either of us will be in the future, but I promise that if you want to talk, I'll listen."

He stared back at her for a long minute, his expression completely unreadable.

After a moment, she changed the subject. "How's your leg now?"

"It will be all right in a minute."

"You were practically running down the beach. Why the big hurry?"

"I don't know."

She didn't believe him. "Really? You don't know? Because I have a theory."

"I'm guessing you're planning to share it with me," he said dryly.

"Being on this beach made you think about the past, and you didn't want to. You thought you could outrun your thoughts – the way you used to do. When we came here as kids, I could always tell when you were worried about your dad, because you always wanted to race me somewhere."

"Maybe I just liked to run."

"You know I'm right."

"You always think you're right."

"Well, I usually am," she said.

His expression lightened. "I don't remember you being this cocky, Alexa."

"I grew into it." She paused, meeting his gaze. "You don't have to pretend with me, Braden. You can just be who you are, say what you think, the way you used to. We talked a lot in those days."

"You talked. I listened."

"You talked some, too. It wasn't all one-sided. You can try to shut me down now, but you can't rewrite history."

"Maybe we just remember our history differently."

"Possibly," she conceded. "We can start from now. I'd like to get to know you again. Why don't you give me a chance?" She got to her feet and offered him a hand. "Don't be proud. Take it."

As soon as he put his hand in hers, she realized her mistake, because the heat of his fingers sent a little tingle down her spine. And when Braden stood up, he didn't let go of her hand. He just stared down at her the way he had all those years ago... Her breath caught in her throat.

Instead of kissing her, he turned and pulled his hand away.

That was fine, she told herself, trying to calm her suddenly pounding pulse. The last thing she needed to do was kiss him again, because just like before, she was leaving in a few days.

Chapter Six

Braden couldn't believe he'd almost kissed Alexa. What the hell was he thinking? He was not in a place in his life to get involved with anyone, much less Alexa. He'd already wasted too many years thinking about her. And despite the fact that it was good to see her again, their lives were going in opposite directions, just the way they always had.

He took the rest of the beach at a slower pace, still feeling tightness in his quadriceps muscle as he walked. Alexa was right about one thing; he hated to feel weak. He'd always been physically active, and after joining the Army, he'd become exceptionally fit. Now he felt like a shadowy version of himself, and he didn't like it. He needed to get his act together, start moving forward. He'd been licking his wounds for too long.

"Oh, look," Alexa said, stopping abruptly. She squatted down and pulled out a beautiful piece of light blue glass. "This is pretty."

"Like your eyes," he said, the words coming out before he could think better of them.

Her cheeks flushed a little. "Maybe I'll take this with me," she said, as she stood up.

"And do what with it? You're an accountant now." He still couldn't believe his once imaginative and creative friend had ended up in a job where she punched numbers all day long.

"I don't know what I'll do with it," she murmured, slipping it into the pocket of her jeans.

"Maybe it will remind you of who you used to be," he said pointedly.

"Do you think I need reminding?"

"Do *you* think you need reminding?" he countered.

She frowned. "I hate people who answer questions with questions. It reminds me of the psychiatrist my mom used to make us see."

"You saw a shrink?"

"It was part of family counseling, although my Dad only went once, so it wasn't much of a family experience."

"Did it help to talk things out?" He'd had his own sessions with an Army psychiatrist and hadn't found them at all helpful. However, if he were honest, the lack of progress was most likely his fault. He'd gone under duress, and hadn't been willing to open up.

"It didn't help me," Alexa said. "My mom might have gotten something out of it. She loved to talk about how badly my dad had treated her, and the doctor was paid to listen. She got to vent to her heart's content. The only other person she had to talk to was me, and I wasn't much help. I was a kid. I didn't know what to say. I just knew I had to keep things together until she got back on her feet."

"That was a big burden, feeling responsible for someone else's happiness," he said quietly. "Especially when that someone was your mother. It's supposed to be the other way around."

"It was what it was. I just had to keep putting one foot in front of the next. I couldn't let myself look too far forward, because I'd trip."

He was beginning to understand a little better why she'd lost contact with him and why she'd stopped dreaming. Her reality had been too much to deal with. She'd had her hands full with her mother.

He just wished she would have confided in him. Then she would have had someone to vent to, and maybe he could have helped.

Alexa paused as they reached the stairs leading up to the Wellbourne house. "Here we are."

He glanced up at the castle-like house that dominated the bluff. Two stories tall, wide and sprawling with a turret and a widow's walk, the house was as intriguing and majestic as it had always been. He hadn't spent much time on this part of the beach after Alexa left. It had made him miss her too much.

The gate leading to the cement stairs was open, so they climbed the three flights to the top of the bluff.

"Do you think the house is empty?" she asked.

"I would imagine so," he replied. His gaze came to rest on some broken glass beneath a now open window. "But I don't believe we're the first ones here."

"Another break-in," she muttered. "Do you think the police know?"

"I'll call Drew later. We might as well take a look inside first."

"What if the police come and think we're the ones who broke in?"

"We'll convince them otherwise. Come on."

"And you're the one who said I have all the bad ideas."

He grinned. "Well, maybe things have changed a little." Walking over to the window, he brushed away the remnants of glass with the sleeve of his shirt. "I'll go in and then come around and open the door."

He climbed through the window, landing in what appeared to be a den. Ignoring the urge to start investigating, he headed through the room to the front door where Alexa was waiting.

"Wow, it's as grand as I imagined," she said as she stepped inside and looked around the foyer with its two-story high ceiling and spiraling staircase.

"It is impressive," he agreed.

"There's still some furniture here," she said, waving her hand toward a side table.

"I guess they're not completely done clearing it out." He moved toward the den, returning to the room he'd just left. Alexa followed, moving immediately over to the tall bookshelves. There was a pile of scattered books on the floor, as if someone had gone through them quickly.

"Jack liked politics," Alexa murmured as she picked up a presidential biography and set it back on the shelf. "Shipwrecks, too," she added, picking up another volume.

"Maybe just for show," he put in, wandering over to the last remaining picture on the wall. It was an impressionistic oil painting. "I wonder why this didn't make it to your aunt's shop."

"She doesn't do a lot of art," Alexa replied.

He took the picture down, wondering if he'd find something behind it, like a safe, but the wall was solid.

"I am surprised he didn't send over these books," Alexa said. "Look at this." She held up a very worn book. "This is a first edition Nancy Drew.

Her voice filled with excitement, and he smiled. "Sounds more like your taste than Jack Wellbourne's."

"Maybe it belonged to one of his kids or his wife," she added, as she flipped to the copyright page. "It's really old. I wish I could take this with me."

"You probably could."

"Don't be ridiculous. That would be stealing."

Despite her refusal to take the book, she seemed awfully reluctant to put it down.

"We can ask the lawyer," he suggested. "I'm sure they'd agree to give you the book."

"This is silly. I don't need this," she said, finally setting it aside. "It's for a child."

"It's for someone who likes a good mystery, and that would be you."

"Well, right now I'm having my own adventure. I don't need a book."

"It's been a long time since you had an adventure, isn't it?" he asked.

She frowned. "My life is not as boring as you think it is, at least not all of the time. But I must admit I haven't done much more than work the last few months. Let's check the upstairs."

He followed her up the staircase. They walked down the hall and into the master bedroom. The room was enormous with a dark hardwood floor and a massive stone fireplace along one wall. The ceiling was at least fifteen feet high, and the windows offered a fantastic view of the beach. The walk-in closet was empty, but there were two large boxes outside the door that appeared to be filled with clothes and other items. One read *For Charity*, and the other was labeled *Junk*.

While he stopped to look more carefully at the boxes, Alexa walked through the double doors leading to the deck.

"Braden," she called a minute later. "Check this out."

He walked out to join her. The view was even better out here. There was nothing but sand and sea and endless horizon. The neighboring homes were also large, but were set back, so there was nothing to obstruct the view. He'd never really seen the beach they'd roamed from this vantage point. He'd always been on the sand looking up.

"This is where we used to see Shayla," Alexa said. "I can see her in my mind, her white dress, her long red hair. She would pace back and forth, as if she were waiting for someone. She seemed lonely. But everything I read indicated she was quite popular, especially with men. I wonder why she spent so much time here. Was she sad about something? Hiding out for some reason?"

"Maybe from the reviews on her last movie," he said.

"That was probably disappointing," Alexa agreed. "She was used to success, to getting what she wanted. It must have been a little shocking to fail."

"I'm sure she had plenty of people to comfort her."

"We need to find out who was here with her that night, Braden. I wonder who rented the house, if it was through the Wellbournes directly or some kind of rental agency?"

"My sister works for a real estate company. It's the largest one in town, so it's possible it was the one the Wellbournes used," he said. "Carey might be able to help. But even if there's a record of Shayla renting the house, we still won't know who was visiting her."

"Unless there's another name on the rental."

"It's something to check out. But which mystery are we solving – Shayla's death or who broke into your aunt's antique store?" It was clear to him that Alexa was caught up in Shayla's mysterious death.

"I'd like to solve both. And I just have this strange feeling they're somehow connected." She gave him a self-conscious smile. "I know it's probably my imagination looking for a story where there isn't one."

"Probably," he agreed.

"But you're not trying that hard to stop me."

He smiled back at her. "I'm curious, too."

"I'm glad you're admitting it."

"And I didn't have anything better to do today."

He walked back into the bedroom, and Alexa followed. He glanced through the box designated to go to charity and found mostly clothes. He checked through the pockets of some discarded jeans and jackets, not expecting to find anything, so he was stunned when his fingers closed around a cylinder. Pulling it out, he realized it was an old roll of film.

"Look at this -- undeveloped film," he said, a shot of energy shooting through his body. He'd thought this search was pointless. It was just something to do while he spent more time with Alexa, but now...

Alexa's eyes sparkled with excitement as she came over to him. "I wonder what's on the roll."

"Only one way to find out. We'll get it developed."

"Before we turn it over to the police?"

"Drew asked me to help with the investigation. Let's see if it's worth reporting."

"I can't wait to see what's on it," she said. "Is there somewhere in town we can get it developed quickly?"

"The local drug store develops film. Was there anything in the other box?"

"Just bathroom stuff, toothbrush holder, soap dish, that kind of stuff. Nothing as interesting as this."

"It could have nothing to do with Shayla. A lot of people were in this house, Alexa."

"I know, but it's fun to imagine." She took one last look around the room. "I wonder what's going to happen to this house now. Will they sell it, or will one of Jack's sons move in?"

"Who knows? It has to be worth a lot of money. I suspect the sons inherited the property."

"Which means they wouldn't have had to break in to see what was here," Alexa said.

"True."

"Which leads me to believe the break-in here and the robbery at the antique store are connected, because as you said before, it's too big of a coincidence."

"It does seem likely," he admitted. "Wellbourne is still the connection, not necessarily Shayla, but definitely Wellbourne."

"Someone wanted something that they didn't have access to while Jack Wellbourne was alive," Alexa said. "We just have to figure out what."

He tightened his hold on the roll of film." Maybe we're getting close."

They moved out of the bedroom and down the stairs, giving the other rooms on the first floor a cursory look before heading outside.

As they walked back down to the beach, he said, "We need to be careful, Alexa. Your aunt already ended up in the hospital. I don't want anyone else to get hurt, especially you."

"I understand. Aunt Phoebe is why I'm doing this. Whoever hurt her needs to pay for almost killing her."

"I just don't want you to pay," he said. "Maybe I should get this film developed on my own."

"Don't be silly. No one saw us go into the house. And no one saw us grab that roll of film."

"I hope not," he said, looking around.

They appeared to be alone on this stretch of the beach, but he couldn't afford not to consider the possibility that someone had seen them go into the house. As soon as he got the film developed, he was going to find a way to pull Alexa back. Maybe if the film turned up nothing, she'd be frustrated enough to quit. But even as the thought crossed his mind, he knew he was being stupid. When Alexa set her mind on something, she didn't quit. It was one of the things he liked most about her.

Chapter Seven

The drugstore was right next to a coffee house, so Alexa and Braden ducked inside while waiting for the film to be developed. Comfortable couches and chairs decorated the upscale interior. Several people were seated at tables working on their laptop computers while a group of women chatted in one corner. After picking up their drinks, they took a seat at a table by the window.

"The town has really grown since I was last here," Alexa commented. "New buildings, more people. It's not even summer, but the streets are already crowded."

"Technology lets people work from anywhere," Braden said, tipping his head to the people working across from them.

"So true. Speaking of work." She took a sip of her latte. "What are you going to do now that you're no longer in the Army?"

Braden sighed as if he couldn't believe she was asking him another question. But instead of completely shutting down, he said, "I have no idea."

"That must be difficult for you," she murmured. "You always knew what you were going to do. You had your life mapped out, and you just had to stick to it."

"Which I did. I just didn't realize the road was going to end this soon."

"What about something with boats? You always liked to sail, and there's plenty of water around here. I bet you could work a charter service or maybe start your own."

"I don't think so."

"You like to eat. Do you know how to cook?"

"Not well enough to cook for anyone else," he said dryly. "I'm a whiz at eggs though. Scrambled, over easy, omelets -- name your favorite egg dish, and I can make it."

She smiled. "You can open a cafe specializing in eggs."

"Somehow, I don't think I would make enough to pay the rent."

"Is there anything else you've thought about doing?" she asked.

"Nothing seriously. I'll figure it out, Alexa."

"I'm sure you will. But I could help."

"You and your bad ideas, I don't think so."

She made a face at him. "Fine, let's talk about something else."

"Now that's a good idea. I guess you were due."

"Ha-ha. How is your Mom doing?"

"She's good." He paused, sipping his coffee. "She's apparently dating. His name is Dale. He runs an auto shop in town."

His words were carefully neutral, and Alexa couldn't help wondering what he thought about his mother having a new relationship. "Do you like him?"

"He seems all right. I don't really know him."

"Is it strange to see your mom with someone else?"

"Everything about my life seems strange," he said with a sigh. "But if she's happy, then I'm happy."

"She has been alone a long time -- more than ten years."

"Yes, she has."

"Hey, maybe you could work for Dale. You could always fix the chain on my bike."

He gave her a look of disbelief. "And that makes you think I could fix cars?"

"You have an aptitude for grease," she said with a smile.

He rolled his eyes. "I don't think so. And I do not have an aptitude for grease. You just didn't like to get your hands dirty."

She grinned at the memory. "You're right. I didn't. Okay, so here's another idea -- what about police work? You said you were in military intelligence, and Drew is obviously happy to have you help out on this case, maybe you could be a cop." As she made the suggestion, she found herself liking the idea. Braden would be a great police officer. He was smart, strong, and he had a tough edge to him, especially now that he'd grown up and served in the military.

"Stop trying to find a job for me, Alexa."

"Come on, think about it. You have an air about you now that says *don't mess with me*. That could work well for you as a cop."

"If that's my air, how come you're messing with me?"

She shrugged. "Because you were once my best friend, and I don't scare that easily. Tell me what you did in military intelligence."

"I can't. It's classified."

"Were you a spy?"

He laughed. "Yeah, I was a spy, just like in the movies. I wore a tuxedo and had a half dozen hot women following me around."

"Well, how would I know what you did? You're very secretive. That would make a good trait in a spy," she added.

"Maybe you should be in police work. You're very good at interrogation," he said.

"I could never be a detective. I would get too caught up in the most intriguing and probably outlandish scenario."

"Well, at least you have some self-awareness," he said dryly.

She smiled, liking the fact that they'd somehow ended up on a more even keel. In fact, the last few minutes of conversation had made her feel like she was really talking to her best friend again.

"I am now more curious about what you did in the service," she said.

"I didn't think it was possible for you to be more curious," he said. "And you became an accountant – really?"

"Stop questioning my choice of career. Accounting can be very interesting. Figuring out where the money came from and where it went can be just as big a mystery as anything else."

"It's just not you, Alexa. You were never about math and numbers. You told stories, you collected sea glass, you wanted to be a glassmaker."

She was surprised and touched that he remembered that. "Childhood dreams, Braden. When I grew up, I needed a job that was stable and that paid well. I wanted things to add up, to make sense, and there was a comfort to working with numbers. There weren't as many variables." She sounded incredibly boring, she realized, but at least she wasn't drowning in a world of chaos anymore.

A gleam of understanding entered his eyes. "I actually do get it, Alexa. Now that you've told me more about how unsettling your life was after the divorce, I can understand why you felt you had to protect yourself and create a stable world to live in."

"I'm glad you understand," she said, relieved she wasn't going to have to defend her job anymore, because since talking to Braden, she'd begun to realize just how far she'd drifted from her dreams. And conversations like this one were making her question all of her choices.

"So, you have a good job, what about the rest of your life?" he asked. "Are you seeing anyone?"

"Not at the moment."

"Why not?"

"I've been busy at work. But I've had boyfriends," she added quickly, not wanting him to think she was alone all the time.

"I'm sure you've had a lot of them."

"Just no keepers," she heard herself admitting. "It's my fault. I'm too picky and too scared. I'm not even sure I really want love in my life. It can cause so much pain. I don't want to go through that."

"Not all marriages end in divorce."

"Yours did." She immediately felt bad for the dig, but Braden took the hit with a simple nod.

"You're right. I'm the last person who should be giving advice."

"Evie told me that your wife asked for the divorce when you were in the hospital."

His lips tightened. "I hate that people talk about me."

"Is that what happened? It seems very cold."

"It's not exactly the way it went down."

"Was it a mutual decision then?"

"In the end it turned out to be," he said.

"I guess that makes it easier if you're both on the same page."

"There's nothing about it that's easy, Alexa. I messed up. Kinley did, too. We didn't bring out the best in each other. We brought out the worst. I don't think marriage is supposed to work that way."

"Do you still love her?" The question came out before she could stop it, but once spoken, she really wanted to know the answer.

He didn't reply right away, and then he finally said, "No."

She waited for more of an explanation, but as Braden lifted his coffee cup to his lips, it was obvious he'd said all he intended to say.

"But..." she pressed.

"Alexa, leave it alone."

"I will leave it alone -- in a second. One thing I've always known about you, Braden, is that you're intensely loyal to your friends. You don't walk away from people. So if you're walking away from your marriage, then it had to be bad."

"She walked away first," he said.

"That doesn't sound mutual."

"In the end, it was. She just said the words first. And that's all I'm going to say on the subject."

Alexa sat back in her seat, pondering her next conversational move, when a young woman approached the table.

"Sorry to interrupt," she said, "But I want to invite you to the big fundraiser we're holding for Daniel Stone, candidate for state senator." She handed them a flyer. "We really hope you can come. Mr. Stone is an incredible man. He grew up here in Sand Harbor. Anyway, it's an Open House from 3:00-6:00 on Saturday at the Stone's house on Harbor View. There will be great food, music, and of course a Q&A session, so you can really get to know Mr. Stone. I hope we'll see you there."

"Thanks," Alexa said.

As the volunteer moved on, Alexa glanced down at the photo of the candidate. Daniel Stone was a very attractive man. He appeared to be his late thirties. He had light brown hair and brown eyes and had the look of a man who'd been thoroughly styled for the photo shoot. He also looked familiar. "I think I've seen this guy before."

"Of course you did. We used to call him Harvard and his friend, Yale," Braden said.

She met Braden's gaze. "This is the preppy college guy who had all the parties on his father's boat?"

"That's the one."

"I guess he wound up having more ambition than just seeing how many beers he could guzzle in an hour."

"Apparently. I find his fundraiser amusing though."

"Why?"

"Because he was always above everyone. Now, he wants to mingle with the little people?"

"Well, now he's trying to get votes."

"Exactly. You know, Daniel Stone is probably the same age as Jack Wellbourne's sons," Braden added, his expression thoughtful. "I think they used to run around together."

"Back to Wellbourne again. All roads seem to lead us back to him."

"It's a small town. There aren't that many roads."

"True." She set the flyer aside. "Shall we go see if the film is ready?"

He nodded and got to his feet, wincing as he did so. He was obviously still in some pain, not that he'd admit that to her.

As they moved toward the exit, the door opened and a woman walked in. She was tall and slender with short, straight brown hair, and was dressed in black leggings, a leather jacket and a pair of stylish boots.

Braden stopped abruptly. So did the woman. A tense look passed between them.

"Braden," the woman said in a voice that seemed both angry and uncertain, as if she wasn't quite sure about her reception.

"Kinley," Braden acknowledged tightly.

Kinley's gaze turned to hers. "Who's your friend?" she asked.

"Does it matter?" he countered.

"Just trying to be polite. This is a small town, Braden. We're going to run into each other."

Braden remained silent.

"I'm Alexa Parker," she said, as the woman's gaze turned back to her. "My aunt owns the antique shop."

"You're Alexa?" the woman said, as if the name meant something to her. "Well, I didn't think you could surprise me any more, Braden."

"We were just leaving," Braden said. He pushed past Kinley and out the door, leaving Alexa to follow.

She nodded at Kinley and walked out of the coffee house. Braden didn't say anything as they headed across the street, but she could feel the anger in every inch of his long, lean body. The divorce might have been mutual, but they seemed to have some unfinished business.

When they reached the opposite sidewalk, she grabbed his arm. "Wait."

"What?" he snapped.

"Are you all right?"

"I'm fine. Let's get the photos."

"You don't seem fine, Braden. Obviously, running into Kinley upset you."

He pulled his arm free. "I told you I don't want to talk about her, Alexa."

"If you don't want to talk about her, maybe you should talk *to* her," she said pointedly. "You're both really angry."

"That's usually what happens in a divorce."

"You don't have tŏ tell me that. I was right in the middle of one." And as she said the words, Alexa realized the last thing she needed to be was in the middle of another one. Whatever was going on between Kinley and Braden was between them.

"Kinley and I have nothing left to say to each other, Alexa. Stay out of it. It's not your business." He opened the door of the drugstore and waved her in.

He was right. It wasn't her business, and she had no reason to butt in. Without another word, she headed inside to the photo counter.

* * *

After paying for the pictures, they took the envelope outside and took a seat on a nearby bench. "I feel kind of nervous," Alexa said, as she pulled out the photos.

"I doubt we're going to find some big clue," Braden said.

The first few photos were shadows, blurry shots of a bedroom and what appeared to be a woman on the bed.

"Shayla?" Alexa questioned.

"It's really hard to tell," Braden murmured.

Most of the shots were over-exposed, and Alexa began to think there wasn't going to be anything helpful until she reached the last two photos. The setting was the deck of the Wellbourne house. It was evening. A small table was set for what appeared to be a romantic dinner. There were flowers and wine glasses. But who was sharing the dinner?

She turned to the last photo. There was now a birthday cake on the table, and a bunch of lit candles on the cake. There was the shadow of someone's shoulder, someone's red hair – Shayla probably. Her gut tightened. Frowning, she felt as if she were missing something that was right in front of her. "It looks like it's her birthday."

"We should find out when she was born. That might help us date these photos," Braden suggested.

"Not that it matters. They don't tell us anything."

Her gaze moved across the photo once more. Her heart skipped a beat. Next to the cake was a shiny gold lighter with initials on the front. They were too tiny to read, and it was crazy to think that...

"Oh, my God," she whispered.

"What?" Braden asked. "What's wrong?"

She couldn't find the words, didn't want to finish the thought in her head, but she also couldn't look away from that lighter.

Her hand started to shake, and Braden grabbed the photo. "Alexa? What do you see that's so upsetting?"

She met his gaze. "The lighter."

"What about it?"

"It looks just like the one my father had."

His eyes widened with surprise. "Your father? What are you talking about? There must be a million lighters that look like that, Alexa."

"Including his," she said. "My Uncle Stan gave my dad an engraved lighter as a wedding gift. My father used to sneak cigarettes on the back deck when my mother wasn't looking. I watched him light up a hundred times."

"You're taking a big leap. How would your father's lighter have ended up in the Wellbourne's house?"

"Is it that much of a stretch? My father grew up here. He had friends here. In fact, he's only a few years younger than Jack Wellbourne."

"Whoa, slow down," Braden said.

His words barely registered. Her stomach turned over, as her thoughts moved from the lighter to the last few weeks they'd spent in Sand Harbor as a family. There had been so many arguments, so many times her father had walked out of the house to return hours later with no explanation of where he'd been.

"That last summer," she said aloud, "my dad would come down for three-day weekends, but something would always go wrong. My parents would fight, and then he'd take off late at night. Sometimes he didn't come back until the morning."

"You need to take a breath," Braden advised.

"What if he was seeing Shayla? Maybe he was having an affair with her." She clapped a hand to her mouth, feeling like she might be sick.

"Or maybe that lighter didn't belong to your father, and there's absolutely no connection," Braden said firmly.

"My mother accused my father of having affairs."

"Here in Sand Harbor?"

"Maybe. I'm not sure." She paused, finally taking a breath. "Do you really think I'm jumping to conclusions, Braden?"

"Yes. We can't see the initials on the lighter, nor do we know when the photo was taken, if your father was even in town that night."

"Right. We need to find out Shayla's birthdate." She pulled out her phone and opened up the Internet. It didn't take more than a minute to get the date she needed -- which was August 18th. She looked back at

Braden. "Shayla would have celebrated her birthday two days before I left that summer. And my father was in town then."

He shook his head. "I can see how things are adding up in your head, Alexa. But you're still missing a lot of facts. You could probably get answers to some of your questions by talking to your parents."

The idea of talking to her mother about a possible affair her father had had while they were still married was not at all appealing. Her mother had made tremendous strides the last few years, putting her problems behind her, and Alexa didn't want to take her back to that painful place for no reason. Which left her dad. She already had a call into him, and surely he would call back to find out about her aunt's condition. In fact, it seemed odd that she hadn't heard from him yet.

"Alexa?" Braden queried.

She realized she'd been silent for a while. "I need to think about it."

"Good idea." Braden put a comforting hand on her thigh. "We could just drop this whole thing right now. Your aunt is going to be all right. And whether or not the robbery is ever solved, it's doubtful that the antique store will be a target again. If they haven't come back by now, they probably aren't coming back. As for Shayla's death, it happened a very long time ago."

"I can't just stop, Braden. I have too many questions. And I'm not convinced that the antique store won't be a target again, because we don't know if the thieves were interrupted by my aunt and didn't get what they were looking for. Maybe they're just biding time until I go home or there's less police attention on the shop."

He frowned. "You may not like the answers you get to your questions, Alexa. Believe me, I have personal experience in that area."

His cryptic words made her tilt her head. "Are you talking about Kinley now?"

He stiffened. "Never mind."

"No, you opened the door."

"And now I'm closing it."

She ignored him. "What's Kinley like? I could see she's very pretty, but what does she do? Does she have a job? Did you ever talk about having children?"

"What part of *I don't want to talk about her* don't you understand?" he asked in frustration.

"You need to talk, Braden. You've already admitted to hiding out in your apartment, not going into town, not spending time with your family. You have a festering wound, and it needs air, attention."

"From you?"

"Why not me? There was a time in our lives when we talked about everything. And I'm safe, Braden. I don't know anyone but you. I'm not going to judge, and if I do judge, I'll probably be on your side. Because quite frankly, from what little I've heard about Kinley, she seems like a bitch."

He drew in a long breath and slowly let it out. "Fine, I'll tell you this much. Kinley had a lot of expectations that I couldn't fulfill. She wanted kids in the beginning, but I wasn't ready. So we put it off. According to her, we put everything off. When she wanted to buy a house, I asked her to wait until I was finished with my tour. But my deployment kept getting extended. So she bought the house by herself. When I did come home, we couldn't stop fighting. When I left again, she was lonely. I couldn't win. And Kinley didn't really want to compromise." He paused for a moment. "Last year Kinley had an affair. She fell in love with someone else. She probably wouldn't have told me, but I couldn't stop myself from asking."

Her stomach turned over. "I'm sorry, Braden."

"She wanted to know how I could blame her when we'd spent more time apart than together. And I didn't have an answer."

"Whoa, wait a second," she interrupted. "The answer is that she was married to you, she took a vow to be faithful, not a vow to be faithful as long as she wasn't bored or lonely."

"I thought you weren't going to judge."

"I told you I'd be on your side."

"She was alone a lot, Alexa. She didn't expect that."

"She should have known that marrying a soldier would mean being on her own."

"I don't think she thought that far ahead. We were living in the moment, caught up in the fantasy of marriage. The reality wasn't what either of us expected."

"When did you find out about the affair?"

"After I was injured. I was in the hospital. She was standing out in the hall, talking to her sister, saying she didn't know what she should do, because it was going to look bad for her to leave me now that I was hurt, now that I was a hero." He said the word sneeringly.

"It didn't just look bad; it *was* bad," she said. "Kinley should have tried harder."

"Come on, Alexa. You saw your parents go through a divorce. If one person falls out of love, it's over."

Her heart broke for Braden. Despite his pragmatic words, she could hear the pain in his voice. "She was wrong to cheat on you. If she was unhappy, she should have left the marriage first."

"She said she didn't want to leave me when I was in a war zone. She didn't want to put that burden on me when I needed to focus on staying alive."

"That sounds like an excuse."

"It doesn't matter. We weren't right for each other and even if she hadn't cheated, we probably wouldn't have been able to stick together now."

"Why not?"

"Kinley says I'm too dark for her. She sees things in my eyes that scare her."

"That's ridiculous. I'm looking at you right now, and I'm not scared."

He met her gaze. "Kinley wasn't entirely wrong. The things I've been through – they changed me."

She didn't want to diminish what he was saying by trying to make him feel better with false platitudes. Maybe he had changed. Maybe he was still working his way through the darkness he'd been through. But she would never have turned her back on him the way Kinley had done. She would have tried to help.

"Thanks for telling me," she said. "I know you didn't want to."

"You always had a way of getting things out of me."

"You weren't so bad yourself."

They sat for a moment, looking out at the street, but she doubted either one of them was seeing anything but their thoughts.

He suddenly stood up. "I should get going. I have some things to do."

"Things that just came up because you don't want to talk to me anymore?"

He stared down at her, an odd expression in his eyes. "It's not that I don't want to talk to you, it's that I want to talk to you too much. We're falling back into old habits, Alexa, and I need to remember that you're leaving in a few days."

"I'm not gone yet," she said, as she stood up. "I like talking to you, too, Braden. I've missed our conversations. I've missed you." The words slipped out before she could stop them.

"This isn't going anywhere. I want to help you find out what happened in your aunt's shop and maybe with Shayla, but that's it. I don't have anything else to offer."

She had a feeling he was talking to himself as much as he was talking to her. "Let's just take it one day at a time."

"I don't want you to get the wrong idea."

"I'm not getting any idea."

"Of course you are. You always have ideas. When we were at the beach earlier, you looked at those kids' bikes and you remembered."

She met his gaze. "Our first and only kiss. Yes, I did remember. I didn't think you did."

"I've never forgotten."

"It was good." She paused. "Did you ever think about doing it again?"

"Only every minute of every day for about the first three years that we were apart," he admitted.

"Me, too," she admitted. "I didn't know what to do with all those feelings I had."

The tension between them turned electric. The surroundings faded into the background. All she could see was Braden, his green eyes, his strong jaw, his full lips. She didn't know who moved first, but suddenly his mouth was on hers. And this kiss wasn't the tentative caress of an unsure boy but a hot, sexy and demanding kiss from a man who knew exactly what he wanted.

She kissed him back with the same fervor, one

touch leading into another and another. She could feel his heat down to the tips of her toes. And when he put his arms around her and pulled her in close, she went willingly.

His tongue slipped past her parted lips, sweeping the cavern of her mouth, making her body ache for even closer contact.

She didn't want it to end.

But it did.

Braden suddenly lifted his head and jerked back a step, his hands falling from around her body, his breath coming rough.

Her heart was pounding as if she'd sprinted a few miles in the last few seconds. She wasn't sure she could catch her breath to speak. If she could speak, what would she say?

Braden answered the question by leaving. She thought about going after him, but she couldn't move.

She'd never had a kiss that had moved her like that. It certainly hadn't been anything like the last one they'd shared. But she had a feeling it would be just as difficult to forget.

Chapter Eight

Was he completely out of his mind? Obviously the answer was yes.

Braden's heart began to slow down as he tried to walk off Alexa's kiss. She certainly hadn't kissed like that when she was twelve. She'd been so sensual, so passionate. And she'd tasted even better than he remembered. He blew out a breath, telling himself not to get carried away. It was just a kiss. A really good kiss. But it wasn't like he'd never had one before.

He needed to get a hold of himself. It was only natural that they would kiss again. They'd been taking a walk through the past all day. It was inevitable they'd end up back in each other's arms. But this kiss wasn't a goodbye kiss. Alexa wasn't leaving in the morning. He would have to see her again. He would have to keep his hands off her. He would have to make sure that he never ever kissed her again.

He couldn't take her into the darkness with him. Maybe if they'd gotten back together in high school or after college. Maybe if he hadn't married someone else or gone to war. But he couldn't change what he'd been through or the man he'd become. The last thing he needed to do was drag Alexa down into the abyss with him.

He needed her to stay that beautiful, golden girl from his childhood, but a part of him knew it was already too late for that to happen.

He shouldn't have kissed her.

She shouldn't have kissed him back.

His mental rant continued with a new subject – Alexa. He'd told her about his divorce, his injuries, his mental and physical scars. She should have been running for home. She'd admitted to him that she was scared of love, that she didn't want to invest in someone who could break her heart. And there was no doubt in his mind that he could do exactly that. Because he wasn't the boy she'd had a crush on. They both needed to remember that fact.

Turning at the next corner, he knew that there was really only one way to end their relationship and that was for her to leave. But that wouldn't happen until they figured out who had broken into the antique shop. Now, having seen that lighter in the photo, Alexa probably wouldn't go until she figured out whether or not her father had been having an affair with Shayla Cummings. He didn't want to believe that Alexa's father was connected to Shayla, but from what he knew of Rob Parker, it wasn't outside the realm of possibility. He needed to get Alexa answers, so they could both return to their lives.

Ignoring the cramping muscle in his leg, he jogged up the stairs to the front door of the police station and headed inside.

Drew was in the middle of a conversation with another officer. He waited for them to finish and then joined Drew at his desk. "I went by the Wellbourne house," he said. "I found another broken window. Looks like someone wanted to take a look around there, too."

"Damn. I checked the house yesterday, and everything was locked up tight," Drew said.

"Well, it's not anymore." He set the envelope of photos on the desk. "I found a roll of film in a woman's jacket inside the house. I got it developed."

Drew frowned. "Excuse me? You searched the house?"

"It was basically empty, and the window was open. I wanted to check things out."

Drew opened the envelope and flipped through the pictures. "This looks like a lot of nothing. What am I missing?"

"The name on the birthday cake is Shayla. She stayed at the Wellbourne house right before she drowned."

"I remember that incident," Drew said, glancing back up at him. "But that was a long time ago. And what does a photo of a birthday cake have to do with anything?"

He couldn't blame Drew for his confusion. Drew hadn't been caught up in the past like he and Alexa had been.

"The photo isn't important," he said, not wanting to bring Alexa's father into anything. "But I think Shayla might be. I've done some research on her mysterious death. Cause of death was drowning, no evidence of homicide. However, she was wearing a white gown when she was found, which implies she wasn't just taking a swim. It could have been suicide. This department obviously investigated. I'd like to look at those files."

"What does this have to do with the break-in at the antique store?"

"I think there could be a connection."

Drew gave him a look of disbelief. "You're reaching."

"I'm just getting involved – the way you asked me to," he reminded Drew. "And I'm not on the payroll, so I can reach in any direction I want. Can you pull up the information on the investigation into

Shayla Cummings' death?"

"Doubtful. The department computerized about ten years ago. Earlier files are in storage. It would take some time to find."

"Could that time be mine?" he asked. "Can you get me in there?"

"Seriously? Why are you so interested?"

"It's a loose thread. I'm intrigued."

"And?" Drew asked, giving him a speculative look. "You have to give me more, because I'm not seeing any link at all."

"Shayla is tied up in my past, too," he said. "Alexa and I used to roam that part of the beach below the Wellbourne house. We overheard a fight between Shayla and someone in the shadows. She drowned not too long after that. Alexa and I have been talking a lot about the past, and we both wonder if we witnessed something."

"Did you tell anyone about this fight?"

"No, I was twelve years old and I wasn't paying any attention to what was going on in town."

"That's right. You were moping because Alexa left early that summer." Drew said with a knowing smile.

"Can you get me into storage?" he asked.

"I wanted you to get involved in a recent robbery not a cold case from more than a decade ago. Are you sure you're not trying to solve the mystery of Shayla so you'll have a reason to spend more time with Alexa?"

Drew's sharp eyes saw him a little too well. He didn't want to get into a discussion about Alexa. "I still think there's a connection between the past and present events," he said. "The break-in at the Wellbourne house strengthens my theory."

"It strengthens the connection between the break

in at the antique store and Jack Wellbourne, but I'm not sure it ties into an accidental drowning from a very long time ago."

"Well, we have no other leads, so I'm going to follow the trail and see where it leads. I need something to do. Isn't that why you asked for my help anyway?"

"I told you I'm shorthanded."

"Yeah, right. I believe you're short of help, but I also know you wanted to get me out of the apartment. So I'm out now, and this is what I'm doing."

Drew nodded. "All right. The files are stored in a unit at the Wilkey Storage Center. I believe they're labeled by year so that should narrow the search. I'll leave your name with the manager."

"Thanks," he said, getting to his feet.

"But you could choose an easier path," Drew said.

"What's that?"

"Talk to the Chief. He's been here twenty years. He might remember something. From what I've seen of the old files, there wasn't much in the way of good record keeping."

"Good idea."

"He's been spending a lot of time at the hospital with Phoebe. But if he's not there, you can try him at home." Drew jotted down an address and handed it to him.

As he read the address, he realized how close the Chief lived to Phoebe. "I forgot they were neighbors," he said.

"I think they might be closer than that," Drew said with a grin. "The Chief told me he's thinking about proposing to her."

"They're that close?" he asked. If Chief Hayes and Phoebe were good friends, maybe the Chief had

purposefully kept Rob out of any investigation into
Shayla's death. As his mind leapt ahead, he realized
he was getting as bad at jumping to conclusions as
Alexa. But at least he had one more person to talk to,
and one more question to ask.

"The Chief spends a lot of time with Phoebe,"
Drew replied. "He takes her out on his boat on
Saturdays all the time. I could see them getting
together, and I think it would be great." He got to his
feet. "Do you want to grab some lunch?"

"No, but I'll take a ride home if you're going
out."

"How did you get here?"

"I walked."

"All the way from your apartment?"

"No, I was with Alexa," he said.

"With Alexa," Drew mused with a lazy grin.
"Interesting."

He shook his head. "It's not what you think."

"You don't know what I think."

"I have a fairly good idea. We're just friends.
That's it."

"If you say so."

"I do say so."

"But why?" Drew asked. "Does she have a
boyfriend? Is there something wrong with her?
What's the deal?"

He thought for a long moment, wanting to come
up with a good excuse, but nothing came to mind. So
he told the truth. "She doesn't have a boyfriend, and
there's not one damn thing wrong with her."

"So what's the problem?" Drew asked.

"She scares the hell out of me. She gets too
close. She digs in. She brings back a lot of memories,
both good and bad. She's just too much."

Drew laughed. "I have a feeling Alexa is just

what you need."

* * *

Alexa stood at the foot of her aunt's bed. Phoebe had had a stream of visitors since she'd arrived a half hour earlier, the latest the Chief of Police, Edwin Hayes. Tall and thin with pepper gray hair, and a commanding presence, Edwin seemed quite taken with her aunt. He'd brought a huge bouquet of flowers and ever since he'd arrived he couldn't seem to take his eyes off of Phoebe.

Unfortunately for Edwin, her aunt seemed to have a few other admirers as well. Butch Hanley from the local hardware store had dropped off her favorite cookies and Ian Holmes, a dashing older man with an Australian accent had brought her a lovely light sweater to wear over her hospital gown.

As Alexa watched Phoebe with her friends, she felt a little envious. Phoebe had so many people who cared about her. Alexa couldn't imagine she'd have more than one or two visitors if she ended up in the hospital. She had girlfriends of course, and she had dates, too, but no special man. As she'd told Braden, she was a coward when it came to love. She didn't want to put her heart on the line for just anyone and so far no one had really tested her resolve – until now.

Her lips were still tingling from Braden's kiss earlier. But he'd also made it clear that he didn't want a future with her. Talk about sending mixed messages. Not that she wasn't conflicted herself. She didn't have any more faith in a future between them than Braden did. She was almost afraid to even think about it.

She'd always had a dream of ending up with Braden, but that had been the dream of a young girl.

Maybe their love seemed more romantic and bigger than life because it had ended so abruptly. If she hadn't been ripped away from Sand Harbor, their feelings probably would have run their natural course. They might have gone out the next summer. Maybe even dated for a few years. But then they would have grown up and away from each other. That was what happened most of the time with most people.

She needed to get over the idea of finding a happily ever after with Braden. Because if she didn't, she was never going to find it with anyone else. She had to let him go.

Or, she had to find out if there was anything serious between them. She couldn't keep thinking of him as some distant possibility. They were both in the same place right now. Where they'd been – where they were going – was not important. The present was all that mattered.

Could she get Braden on board? Could she persuade him to give whatever was happening between them a chance to grow, to flourish? It seemed doubtful.

He'd stormed off after their kiss. As a young girl, she would have taken that to mean he hadn't enjoyed the experience. But she was a woman, and she was old enough to know there was nothing about that kiss he hadn't liked.

There was nothing about that kiss she hadn't liked, either.

But Braden was going through a lot of emotions right now, his failed marriage, leaving the Army, his injuries and whatever had happened to him overseas. This wasn't a good time for him to jump into another relationship. She understood that. But she was afraid if she left now, if they put it off again, they'd never find a way back together.

Was that a risk she wanted to take?

As her mind tumbled over the possibilities, Edwin Hayes came over to speak to her, and she was relieved by the interruption. Maybe some time would clear her muddled thoughts.

"Phoebe is so happy you're here," Edwin said with a friendly smile. "She talks about you all the time. Do you know that every Christmas she buys you an ornament, the way she used to do when you were a child?"

Alexa was stunned. "Are you kidding me?"

He smiled. "She has them all tucked away to give to you one day."

"That's so thoughtful."

"That's the kind of person your aunt is."

"I missed her a lot over the years. I had many happy memories here in Sand Harbor at her house."

"I'm glad you're back now. I hope you won't be a stranger."

"I'm going to try harder not to be." Even though she'd reconnected with her aunt six years ago, she hadn't made the trip back to town until now. Part of that was because of Braden. She hadn't wanted to run into him or his wife. She'd wanted to have her own life settled before that happened. But her strategy of putting things off for another day had never worked very well. Maybe she should make a change. Grab what she wanted and hold on tight.

"Is your father here, too?" Edwin asked.

His question brought her back to the present. "No, I haven't been able to reach him."

"Did you tell him how badly injured your aunt was?" Edwin asked with annoyance.

"I've left several messages to that effect."

Edwin's lips drew tight, and he gave her a

disgusted look. "I always knew Rob was selfish, but I thought he cared about Phoebe. She did so much for him when he was a young man. I'm sorry if I'm insulting your father, but I just don't understand him."

She couldn't defend her dad. He was selfish. She was just a little surprised that Edwin Hayes knew it, too. Her father had a very charming side as well, and most people thought he was a great guy – at least those people who didn't live with him. Although, he seemed pretty happy with his second wife.

"Well, I hope to see you again," Edwin said, extending his hand.

She shook his hand. "I hope so, too."

"Don't be in a rush to leave," he added. "Your aunt likes to pretend she's strong and independent, but she needs her family around, and she's shaken by what happened at her shop. She loves that place; it's her second home. I can't believe she almost..." He couldn't bring himself to say the word. "It shouldn't have happened."

"No, it shouldn't have," she said.

"I'm staying on top of the investigation," he said. "I've got everyone available working on the case."

"I know. I appreciate that."

As the Chief left, she walked to the side of the bed, exchanging smiles and goodbyes, until she was alone with her aunt.

"You're quite popular," she said, taking a seat in the chair by the bed. "And here I was worried you were going to be alone all day."

"Small towns are all about community," Phoebe said. "I do love my friends."

"And they love you. Especially the Chief of Police. He seems quite taken with you."

Her aunt gave her a little smile. "I've known Edwin almost twenty years. He had a lovely wife, too, but she didn't care for his workaholic tendencies, and they divorced."

"I can't imagine being a workaholic in Sand Harbor."

"That's because you always vacationed here. But the people who live here year round work hard to make that happen."

She nodded. "I'm sure that's true."

"Edwin came from nothing, so he had to work harder than most. He did really well for himself, though, and he runs this town like a finely tuned clock. He can't believe what happened to me."

"I'm sure he'll do everything he can to solve this case."

Phoebe smiled. "I'm sure he will." She paused. "He asked me to marry him a few months ago."

"Wow, what did you say?"

"That I would think about it."

"Do you love him?"

"I do care about him, but it's so difficult for me to think of marrying again. I loved my husband so much. I don't know that I can give that kind of love to anyone else. Anyway, don't say anything. No one else in the family knows."

"I won't." She paused. "I don't think Chief Hayes is the only man who is smitten with you."

Her aunt blushed. "Oh, Butch and Ian are just dear friends."

"I think you can have your pick, so you should take your time, figure out what or who you really want."

"That's good advice. So tell me, what did you do today, Alexa?"

"I wasn't as productive as I should have been," she admitted. "I mostly wandered around town and the beach." She didn't want to bother her aunt with any of her crazy theories about the break-in until she knew if one of them was true. "When I leave here, I'm going to dig into those boxes at the antique shop and get everything organized for you."

"Don't work too hard. You should have some fun while you're here. Maybe get to know Braden again," her aunt added with a sly smile. "It was so fun to see the two of you together."

"Don't match make," she warned.

"Why not? You loved him once."

"When I was twelve."

"Well, you're still single. And Braden is getting divorced. It seems to me like you two are finally in the right place at the right time. I know when you came to see me after college that you were hoping to see him, too."

"We'll see what happens," she said. "Helping you is my first priority."

"That's very thoughtful of you, Alexa. I hope you won't be bored."

"Not a chance. I always liked your shop."

"You used to make up stories about the furniture," her aunt said.

"I think that was you, Aunt Phoebe," she replied, as they shared a warm smile.

"Both of us," Phoebe said. "I always had the idea that you might one day come to work with me. Or that I might leave you the shop." She gave Alexa a speculative look.

Alexa was touched by the thought. "I don't know anything about antiques."

"I could teach you." Phoebe paused. "But I know you have your own life. I just wish you were closer. We missed so many years, and now I want to make up for lost time."

"Well, we're making up some of that time now,"

she said, also feeling a twinge of guilt. "I'm glad you're feeling better. Have you remembered anything else about what happened the other night?"

Phoebe shook her head. "No, I wish I could. Edwin keeps asking me, and Officer Lassen came by again this morning, as well. I try to remember, but nothing comes into my mind. I feel like it's right there, but I can't see what it is."

"Well, that's okay. Don't stress out about it." Maybe it was good that her aunt couldn't remember and all her friends knew that. News would get around town, and hopefully her aunt would be less of a target.

"I can't help but wonder what the thief took. I want to get back to my shop, but the doctor says I need to stay here for a few more days. I feel so helpless."

"You can't worry about it right now. You need to concentrate on getting better. The police are investigating, and Braden and I are looking into some things, too."

"You and Braden. It has a good ring to it. I've been worried about Braden. He's been through a lot, and I think he needs support, but he's stubbornly independent. The two of you had a special friendship. Maybe you can break through his walls."

"He's not really interested in my help. As you said, he's stubborn."

"Well, you can be persistent, too. See if you can get him to open up."

"I don't know if I can -- or if I want to. I'm afraid I'll be taking the lid off Pandora's box."

Phoebe smiled. "Sometimes you have to take a risk. And you have to make time, too. Every time I ask if you have a boyfriend, you tell me that you don't have time for love. You need to make it a priority, or you'll end up alone."

"Falling in love doesn't mean I won't end up alone. Look at my mom. Now Braden. There are millions of divorces every year. I don't really know why anyone gets married."

"Because they want to commit to each other. I had a beautiful, strong marriage. I wish you could have known your uncle. Charles was an amazing man. He was strong and kind and intensely loyal."

"He sounds amazing. I haven't met many men like that."

"Braden fits the description."

"Maybe," she conceded. "But his walls aren't going to come down in a day, so let's talk about something else. Let's talk about you."

"I'm fine. I'm getting better. In fact, I'm starting to feel bored."

"Boring is good. That means you're resting."

"I'm trying. I'm not used to being in bed all day." She paused for a moment. "Have you spoken to your father yet?"

"No, not yet. I'm sorry."

"Well, he's busy."

"Yes, he's always been busy," she said, unable to keep the bitterness out of her voice.

Her aunt's gaze narrowed. "He hurt you. I'm sorry about that."

"We don't need to talk about him."

"Sometimes I'd like to kick his ass, the way I used to when he was a kid. My little brother can be very selfish."

"In my opinion, he could use an ass kicking," she said.

"Do you talk to him much?"

"Hardly at all. But I will call him again. Dad should be here for you. You're his only sister, and you did so much for him."

"That's why I'm here," a man said from behind her.

Alexa was shocked to see her father walk into the room. It had been a year since she'd seen him briefly after the birth of his youngest child, and he hadn't changed much. He looked a bit older, but it was clear that he was still a perfectionist when it came to his appearance. His hair didn't show a hint of gray, and his black slacks and button-down shirt didn't boast one wrinkle. The only thing marginally different about him was a slight receding of his hairline.

He smiled at her, then brushed past her to kiss his sister on the cheek. "I'm sorry this happened to you, Phoebe. How are you feeling?"

"I'm a lot better today, Rob. My head doesn't hurt as much. I'm so glad you came. I know how busy you are with your job and the kids."

"I apologize for not getting here sooner. But I know Alexa has been taking good care of you."

"Of course she has."

"I understand you interrupted a robbery. Did you see who did this to you?" her dad asked.

"No. If I did see someone, I don't remember. I have a concussion."

"Do the police have any suspects?"

"No."

"Do you have any idea why someone would break into your shop? Did you get something valuable in?"

Alexa was surprised at her father's sharp interrogation. Wasn't it clear that Phoebe had no idea what had happened?

"My shop is filled with valuables," she said a little tartly. "I don't understand why most people don't realize that."

"Sorry, I didn't mean to upset you."

"How are the children, Rob? You haven't sent me any pictures in a while. They must be getting very big."

As Alexa listened to her father talk about her half-siblings, she felt very disconnected from him. Over the years she had loved him and hated him, and now she felt almost ambivalent, as if he were a stranger.

"Alexa?" he queried.

"Sorry, what did you say?" she asked, realizing her father and aunt were both giving her an expectant look.

"Phoebe says you're helping her with the shop for a few days," her dad said.

She nodded. "Yes, there are a lot of boxes to unpack."

"I'm not leaving until tomorrow, so I can help you."

She was shocked by the offer. "Really?"

"Sure, why not?"

"Okay, I guess so," she said, stumbling a little over the words. The idea that she and her dad might spend a few hours together seemed unimaginable.

"I want to stop by the police station first," her dad continued, "But I can come by the shop after that."

"All right. I'll be there."

"Good."

Her dad smiled at her aunt. "I'll come back later tonight. Try to sleep for a while."

"I will."

He turned to Alexa. "I'll see you in a bit."

"Okay," she replied, still not quite able to believe he was going to help her do inventory at the antique shop.

"That's a first," her aunt commented when they were alone again. "I can't remember the last time Rob even went to my store, much less offered to help out. Your father has a lot of layers."

"What does that mean?"

"Just that he's not all one thing – good or bad."

"I don't really know him, Aunt Phoebe."

"It looks like you're going to get a chance to talk to him. Don't waste it."

"I won't," she said.

There were a few things she wanted to talk to her dad about. She just hoped she could find the courage to ask a question she wasn't sure she wanted the answer to. As Braden had warned, that could be dangerous.

Chapter Nine

After Drew dropped him off at his apartment, Braden picked up his car and headed across town. Edwin Hayes was just pulling into his driveway when Braden parked in front of his house.

He stepped out of the car and called, "Chief Hayes."

Edwin gave him a look of surprise, then crossed the grass to join him on the sidewalk. "Braden? Is that you?"

"Yes it is."

"I heard you're helping us out," the Chief said.

"If I can."

Chief Hayes nodded. "Good. From what I've heard about your military service, we're fortunate to have your help."

"Thanks. Drew thought you might be able to answer a few questions for me."

"Shoot."

"I wanted to know what you could tell me about the drowning death of Shayla Cummings," he said.

Surprise flashed in the Chief's eyes. "I thought you were going to ask me about the crime scene at the antique shop and what I'd seen, but you're asking about a woman who died here a long time ago? Why?"

"There's a link between the Wellbourne delivery and the break-in. I've been researching the Wellbournes and there's one odd note in their history – the fact that one of their renters drowned under somewhat mysterious circumstance." As he stated his theory, he realized how tenuous the link was. The Chief was probably going to regret approving his involvement.

"She didn't die mysteriously; she drowned," Edwin said.

"There was never a thought that it wasn't accidental?"

"Of course there was a thought, but the investigation determined there was no foul play. Her sister said that Shayla couldn't swim very well and also mentioned that she'd been depressed after her movie failed."

"So it could have been suicide?"

"There wasn't a note, but it was a possibility based on what the sister had to say and how Ms. Cummings was dressed. That's why we did a thorough investigation, which resulted in the conclusion that whether it was accidental or deliberate on Ms. Cummings' part, there were no other parties involved in her death."

"Was Shayla a friend of the Wellbournes? Did they have any comment on her death?" he asked, changing the direction of their conversation.

"She had been staying in their house prior to her death, but she was just one of many summer renters."

"Were there many?" he asked doubtfully. "Alexa and I saw her on the deck of that house a lot, but we never saw anyone else."

"I think there were a couple. It was a long time ago." The Chief gave him a thoughtful look. "I had forgotten how close you and Alexa were. I remember the two of you riding your bikes up and down this street every summer."

"We did that a lot."

"I saw Alexa at the hospital a short while ago. It

was good she came back for Phoebe."

"She's worried about her aunt."

"We all are. But you're on the wrong track, Braden. I know it's more imaginative to try and combine mysterious events to each other, but I doubt Shayla Cummings' death has anything to do with the current break-in. You could be wasting valuable time."

"Well, it's not like I'm overlooking any other leads. Let me ask you one more question; did Shayla have any friends in town?" he asked, unwilling to quite let it go yet.

"I recall that she had a few friends, yes."

"I was wondering if I could take a look at the case files, the people you interviewed."

"Well, that would take some effort to find," the Chief said.

"I'd still be interested in looking."

"You'll have to look through the storage unit."

"That's what Drew said." He paused. "What about Rob Parker? Was he friends with Shayla?"

"Phoebe's brother?"

He nodded.

The Chief's heavy brows drew together in a frown. "Well, he was married at the time."

"Married men sometimes cheat."

"I didn't know Rob well, and he wasn't on any interview list that I recall," the Chief said. "What I do know is that Phoebe wouldn't like what you're implying, Braden. And I don't think Alexa would, either."

"Alexa wants to find out what happened at the antique store and to Shayla," he said.

"Even if her father is implicated?"

"You just said Rob didn't know Shayla."

"I said I didn't interview him." He shook his

head. "Maybe it was a mistake getting you involved. You're complicating things unnecessarily."

"I'm just trying to help."

"If you want to help, then stop trying to create a mystery where there isn't one and concentrate on what's happening now. Alexa won't thank you for trying to put her father in the middle of an affair."

"I'm not looking for thanks, just the truth."

"You are covering a lot of bases, I'll say that for you. Do you have any other questions?"

"That's it for now. Thanks, Chief."

As Edwin headed into his house, Braden returned to his car. The Chief had been fairly forthcoming until he'd brought up Rob Parker. It was clear that Edwin was fond of Phoebe and very loyal to her. He wasn't going to provide any information that might hurt the Parker family.

Had the Chief always felt that way? Had he deliberately overlooked a connection between Rob and Shayla just in case there was some tie?

Or was he completely on the wrong track as Edwin had suggested?

Rolling his neck around on his shoulders, Braden considered his options. He doubted the police files would give him more information than the Chief had, and it could take days to even find the case notes. How she died wasn't as important as finding out who was in her life at the time of her death. He needed to find out more about the house rental, and he knew just the person to talk to.

* * *

When Alexa got to the antique store, she found the door open, and her father inside. He was going through one of the boxes on the counter.

"You beat me here," she said, a little surprised. "How did you get in?"

"Evie opened the door for me."

"Oh, I didn't realize she was coming here today."

"There's a shitload of stuff in these boxes," he said.

"And there's a system for organizing," she replied, noting the haphazard collection growing rapidly on the counter.

"Well, I figured I'd just unpack the boxes first, and then it would be easier to see what's here." He took out an old carved box of dominoes. "Most of this looks like crap to me."

"Don't say that in front of Aunt Phoebe," she said.

"I guess it's good she has a store. Otherwise, she'd probably have all this in her house. She's always been a hoarder." He tossed the dominoes back in the box and rifled through a few more items.

"Dad what are you doing here?" Nothing about this moment was adding up. Her father didn't like antiques. He wasn't a big fan of Sand Harbor. And he never had time for anything but his job as a stockbroker. He was always making deals and rarely far from his phone or email.

"I'm helping," he said, glancing back at her. "I told you I would."

"It seems out of character."

"You've always told me I should spend more time with you. This seems like a good opportunity."

"What about your wife, your little kids? Don't you always tell me that they need you more?"

"I can't win with you," he grumbled.

"You never tried to win with me. When you ended your marriage, you ended your relationship with me, too. You divorced me just like you did,

Mom."

He looked surprised that she'd spoken so bluntly. She was a little surprised, too. But she wasn't going to back down. She rarely had the opportunity to speak her mind with her dad, so she might as well use the opportunity to be direct.

"I'm sorry that you felt that way," he said. "It was never my intention to hurt you, Alexa. I wanted the divorce to be amicable, but your mother was so angry with me. I couldn't talk to her for five seconds without her screaming or crying. I just couldn't take it anymore."

"Why didn't you ask for joint custody?"

"Your mom needed you."

"And you didn't," she said flatly.

"It wasn't like that. And you can't pretend you wanted to be with me either. Your mother poisoned your mind. Even when I called, you didn't want to speak to me."

"You rarely called. Don't act like there were dozens of calls that I turned down. The phone only rang on my birthday and occasionally on Christmas, and after a while, not even then."

A grim expression entered his eyes. "I can't go back and change things, Alexa, even if I wanted to."

"It doesn't sound like you *do* want to."

"Some things I would definitely do differently, and that includes spending more time with you," he said. "But I'm not perfect. I make mistakes. Everyone does. All we can do is try to learn from them and move on." He turned back to the box, pulling out a tarnished silver candleholder. "This should probably just go in the trash."

"It can be cleaned up," she said. That was the problem with her father. He was always more interested in throwing things away than trying to fix them.

"If you say so," he muttered, setting it aside.

"Why did you and Mom split up?" she asked abruptly.

He sighed. "Too many reasons to count."

"Was one of those reasons that you were having an affair?"

He jerked at the question, whirling around in surprise. "Why would you ask me that?"

"Because I want to know. It's something I've thought about for a long time. I'm an adult now. I just want an honest answer."

"Did your mother tell you I cheated?"

"I'm asking you, Dad."

He stared back at her for a long moment. "What happened in my marriage is not your business. You're my daughter, Alexa. Some things are private."

She found his reply astonishing. "Some things are private?" she echoed. "Do you have any idea how loud your arguments were? I used to put in my swimming earplugs so I wouldn't have to hear you talk about personal things. I find it odd that you're suddenly so worried about me hearing anything now."

"What's the point? I don't want to drag the past between us yet again. Can't we start from now? You've reconnected with your aunt and your cousin. Let's not go back to all the ugliness. Let's move forward."

"You have to answer my question," she said, ignoring his plea to just move on. "Did you cheat on Mom with an actress named Shayla Cummings?"

He drew in a quick breath. "What do you know about Shayla?"

The way he said her name told Alexa that her father did indeed know the actress. Her stomach grew queasy. Was Braden right? Was she going to hurt herself even more with her endless questions? It was too late to turn back.

"I know she used to rent the Wellbourne's house," she replied. "I know she was fighting with someone a few weeks before she died."

"Where are you going with this?"

"That depends on your answer."

"I don't understand why you're bringing this up now."

"Someone broke into the shop right after these boxes were delivered."

"So?"

"So, there's a mysterious death that could be connected to the robbery."

"I can't imagine how you're putting the two events together. And why would you put me with Shayla?"

She debated for a moment, then said, "I saw a photograph from what appeared to be a birthday party for Shayla Cummings. There was a gold lighter next to the cake. It looked like the one Uncle Stan gave to you."

His jaw dropped. "Are you out of your mind, Alexa? Do you hate me that much that you'd try to make up some story about me and Shayla?"

"It sounds like you knew her."

"You're crazy. This is ridiculous, absolute and utter nonsense."

His tone grew angrier with each word. Alexa's stomach ache increased, the fury in her father's voice reminding her of all those fights she'd overheard when she was a little girl, when she used to pull the covers over her head so she wouldn't have to listen to him yell or hear her mother crying.

As much as she wanted to duck under the covers

right now, she couldn't do that. She needed to stand up to him. "I'm not accusing you of anything. I'm just asking questions, and you're getting defensive. It makes me think you have something to hide."

"I don't recognize you any more," he said with a disgusted shake of his head.

"I wish I didn't recognize you," she returned, feeling overwhelmingly sad. "You always yelled so you wouldn't have to lie. I realize that now. All those fights you and Mom had. You never answered her. You just yelled at her for asking the questions. But I'm not her. I'm not afraid you're going to leave me, because you already did."

His face paled. "I had no idea you hated me so much."

"I wish I did hate you. That would make it easier. But instead I've spent the last fifteen years wishing you'd love me the way you did when I was a little girl. We used to go to Nini's on Sundays for breakfast. I felt so special then." Moisture filled her eyes, and she was angry with herself for still feeling the pain, but she couldn't deny it. "It was our time together. I didn't know that the last time we had pancakes there would be the last time I would *ever* have breakfast with you. I loved you then, and God help me, I still love you now. But you hurt me. And I really hope you don't do the same thing to your other children, because it feels awful." She let out a breath, feeling strangely lighter having said so many of the things she'd always wanted to say.

"I'm sorry, Alexa. I really am."

"I hope you are," she said. "I hope you change."

He stared back at her. "Maybe I should go."

"That's usually what you do." She was disappointed that he wasn't even going to try to convince her she was wrong. But then how could he?

She wasn't wrong about anything, and he knew it.

"Now you sound like your mother," he told her.

"Did you ever love her?" she asked.

"More than I can say," he said with a heavy sigh.

"Really? Then what happened?"

"We weren't right for each other. We wanted different things. I couldn't make her happy. She couldn't make me happy. I know you got caught in the crossfire, Alexa. I didn't handle things as well as I should have. I realize that now."

At least he'd admitted that much.

He stared at her for a long moment. "I knew Shayla Cummings. I was at the Wellbourne house when she celebrated a birthday. It might have been my lighter you saw. But she was just a friend."

"That's it?" she asked.

"I don't want to talk about this with you. You're my daughter. It's not right."

"She was a beautiful young woman and a lot of men wanted her. It's hard to believe you didn't."

"Even if I did, Shayla had her eyes on someone else."

"Who?"

"She was cagey about it. I thought it was Jack Wellbourne, but then Daniel Stone was hanging around, so it could have been him. She didn't want to tell me. She said it made her sad to talk about it."

"Do you think Shayla's death was an accident?"

He didn't answer for a long moment. "I don't honestly know. She used to swim in the early mornings, because she thought she'd gained some weight and she didn't want the paparazzi to catch her in a bikini and point out that not only was she a flop as an actress, she was also getting fat."

"She wasn't wearing a swimsuit when she was found."

"Well, I don't know about that. Maybe she had on a cover-up. Like I said, she was worried about her weight gain."

Alexa wondered about that. In the newspaper photos she'd seen of Shayla, she'd been quite thin, but then models and actresses had a different standard for skinny.

"Shayla had a lot of problems in her life," her father added. "It's possible that depression got the best of her."

"Now you're saying it was suicide?"

"I'm saying I don't know."

"Did you ever talk to the police about her death?"

"No, we were back in Seattle when she died. And your mother and I were in the midst of the divorce. I barely knew what was going on here."

"I'm surprised no one called you. Did no one know of your friendship with Shayla?"

"I wasn't broadcasting it," he said, shifting his feet somewhat awkwardly.

"What about Aunt Phoebe?"

"God, no! My sister is a big talker. I would never tell her anything. And there was nothing to tell. But I can see the suspicion in your eyes now, and I figured that's the same look I'd get from anyone else. Look, I don't believe there's any connection between Shayla's death and the delivery of these boxes. You always had a big imagination. I guess you didn't grow out of it." He paused. "I'll leave you to do the inventory." He moved toward the front door, then turned back and said. "Would you like to have breakfast with me tomorrow before I leave?"

She was shocked at the unexpected question and also surprised that she didn't immediately say yes. Some self-protective mechanism inside her head was making her question if she really wanted to go back to Nini's with her dad. She'd been reliving a lot of her past since she'd returned to Sand Harbor, did she want to revisit that old memory?

"You used to squeal a big yes, with a huge smile on your face when I invited you to breakfast," her dad said, a sad note in his voice.

"I will meet you," she said quietly. "But not at Nini's. Let's go to Hannah's Bagel House."

"All right. Eight o'clock? Is that too early? I need to get back to Seattle by noon to catch my plane."

"It's fine."

"Do you have the photo with my lighter in it?" he asked.

"No, Braden has the pictures."

"Braden? That kid you used to hang around with?"

"That's the one."

"Why does he have the photographs?"

"He's helping me investigate." She noted the look of annoyance in her father's eyes. If he was as innocent as he proclaimed himself to be, why did he care about an old picture of a birthday cake and a lighter that might or might not be his?

"Maybe you could get them back," her dad suggested. "I'd like to take a look."

"I'll see if I can."

"All right. Tomorrow, then."

"Tomorrow," she echoed.

As her father left, she wondered what he was going to do with the rest of the evening. Did he still have friends in Sand Harbor? He hadn't mentioned where he was staying either. She suddenly realized there were a few more questions she could have asked him -- like why he was staying the night at all, if he needed to be back in Seattle by noon on Friday.

He'd already checked in on his sister. What other reason could he have for hanging around until tomorrow?

Chapter Ten

Braden entered the realty office where his sister Carey worked. It was the biggest of three realty companies in Sand Harbor. Carey was one of four associates in the firm. She had received her license six months earlier and was already reaping the benefit of the new developments going up on the outskirts of town.

The receptionist waved him down the hall. Carey was working in the smaller second office on the left. His younger sister took after their fair-haired mother with the same blonde hair, round face and warm smile. Like their mom, Carey was also a hard worker. She'd been working since she was fifteen and loved to make money. She'd told him that love, marriage and family were on the back burner until she'd met her career goals. Maybe she'd learned something from the disaster of his young marriage.

When he entered her office, she looked up from her desk in surprise. "What's wrong?" she asked warily.

"Nothing. Everything's fine."

"Everything can't be fine if you're here. You haven't left your apartment in weeks, nor have you returned any one of my phone calls in the last ten days," she pointed out.

Because her phone calls usually had to do with getting him out of his apartment. "Sorry about that," he muttered. "But here I am."

She tilted her head to one side, giving him a

thoughtful look. "You seem different."

"I didn't come here to talk about me," he said quickly.

"But we need to talk about you. I'm worried."

"You don't have to be. I'm the big brother. It's my job to worry about you, not the other way around."

"That's not the way our family works."

She was right about that. They'd become a very tight unit after his father died – actually, even before his dad had been killed, because it had always been his mom, his brother and his sister. And he'd been the oldest, the one who made sure everyone else was okay.

"I have a question for you," he said, taking a seat in front of her desk.

"What's up?"

"I'm trying to find out who handled the rentals on the Wellbourne estate."

She raised an eyebrow. "Seriously? That's your question for me?"

"Why? What did you think I was going to ask?"

"I don't know. Something more personal -- like, what do you think I should do with the rest of my life? Because I actually have an answer for you."

"What's that?"

"Real estate. This town is booming. It wouldn't take you long to take the classes and we could be partners together. When Matt graduates from law school, we could bring him in on some deal. Make it a family business. It could be great."

He smiled at the enthusiasm in her eyes. "You've thought about this."

"For a long time. The best thing is you'll be safe, and I won't have to worry about the phone ringing in the middle of the night or two men in uniform walking up to our door." Her eyes watered. "I used to dream about that happening, Braden. In my mind, I'd see those guys coming up to the house when Dad was killed, and then I'd think they were coming for you."

He frowned, feeling bad that he'd put her through that. "I never wanted you to worry."

"How could I not? I knew that the worst could happen, because it had already happened once. So..." She cleared her throat. "Back to real estate. We could open our own company and called it C&B Realty."

"You get top billing? I'm the oldest."

"I have the most experience."

"Then you should have your own company."

Her mouth turned down. "Can't you agree to think about it?"

"There's nothing to think about. I'm not interested in real estate."

"It's not a bad job. You can make good money."

"I don't want to sell houses, Carey."

"I guess it would be a little dull when you're used to action."

"I appreciate the thought, really. Now, can we get back to my question? Do you know which company in town handled the rentals for the Wellbournes?"

"Yes, it was us. Mark Bellingham, the owner, was good friends with Jack Wellbourne. In fact, I think Mr. Wellbourne might have actually helped Mark open this company. I know they worked together on several development deals as well."

"That's great. Would you have access to files from fifteen years ago?"

She sat back in her chair and crossed her arms, giving him the same stubborn look she'd given him as a little girl when he'd asked her to do something she didn't want to do. "I need more information about why you're asking."

"I want to find out who rented the Wellbourne house to Shayla Cummings fifteen years ago. It would have been in August or July. I don't know if she was there the whole summer."

"Braden, what are you getting involved in?"

"It's a long story. Can you just help me out here, Carey, without giving me the third degree?"

"I suppose I should be glad you're interested in something," she grumbled.

"Exactly. I'm out of the apartment just like you wanted."

"I wanted you to find something fun to do with your time, maybe have drinks with friends, or go for a bike ride with me."

"Well, that may happen at some point. Right now I'm interested in this."

"Okay, fine." She opened up the computer. "Mark recently had an intern update our file system. I think it goes back that far." She punched in some dates. "Let's see."

He got up and moved around the desk so he could look at the screen.

"It looks like the house was rented for the month of August by Daniel Stone," she said.

His pulse leapt as he followed her gaze to the name on the rental agreement. "Daniel Stone? Why would he rent the house? His parents had their own beach house."

She shrugged. "I don't know."

"Did anyone else rent it that summer?"

She scrolled through several more screens. "It looks like it wasn't rented through this office for the six months prior. But that's not unusual. Summer is when most of the rentals occur."

"What about the previous summer?"

She flipped back to another screen. And there was the name he wanted to see... Shayla Cummings. She'd rented the house for three weeks the previous July in her own name. Why had she come back the next summer and rented under Daniel Stone's name? Had the two of them had a relationship?

"Shayla Cummings is that actress who died on the beach, right?" Carey asked.

"Yes."

Carey gave him another speculative look. "Now, do I get an explanation?"

"I'm helping Drew investigate the break-in at the antique store. It might tie to the Wellbournes."

A gleam came into her eyes. "I heard that Phoebe's niece is back in town. Have you seen her?"

"Yes."

"Now, I get it," she said with a gleeful smile.

He frowned. "You don't get anything."

"She's the reason you're out of the apartment."

"It was Drew who asked for my help."

"Well, whoever it was, I'm glad to see you out and about. I'm so mad at Kinley, and I don't think it's fair that she's still in your house while you're living in that horrible apartment."

"It was my choice, and the place is not that bad." He appreciated his sister's support, but he wanted to keep his divorce between him and Kinley. "It's for the best," he added, realizing as the words came out of his mouth that he actually meant them. "We both need to move on."

"Are you moving on?"

"I'm trying a little harder now," he admitted.

Relief flashed in her eyes. "I'm very happy to hear that. So, what are you doing for dinner tonight?"

"I don't know," he said slowly, thinking about Alexa, wondering whether or not he wanted to meet up with her again.

"We could go out, maybe call Mom to join us," Carey suggested. "Or I could cook."

"You cook?" he asked doubtfully.

"Well, I could order pizza. Or Mom would cook. She's been stacking up casseroles in the freezer ever since you ordered her to stop dropping off food at your apartment."

"I didn't order her to stop."

Carey rolled her eyes.

"Fine, we'll do dinner. Call Mom and tell her to meet us at Rocco's at six. I'll buy."

"Really?" A hopeful smile spread across her face.

"Yes. I'll see you there."

"I'm glad we're doing this, Braden. It's been too long."

"Yeah, it has," he said. "Thanks for the info."

"I hope it helped."

"Well, it gave me something else to think about."

* * *

Alexa had just finished going through the last of the Wellbourne boxes when Braden walked into the antique shop a little after five.

"Hi," she said warily, not sure what mood she'd find him in after the way he'd left her earlier.

"Hey," he returned, glancing at the stack of items on the counter. "Looks like you're making progress."

"Some. I haven't found anything that looks extremely valuable or in any way scandalous or damaging. But at least there will be a little less work for my aunt when she returns."

"Did you see her this afternoon?"

"Yes."

"How was she?"

Apparently, they weren't going to talk about the kiss they'd shared earlier. That was fine with her. "She's getting better by the minute. She still doesn't remember anything about that night. A lot of her friends were there, including the Chief of Police, who assured me he would not rest until he found out who had hurt Phoebe. I think he's in love with my aunt."

"I got that impression, too."

"When did you talk to him?" she asked with surprise.

"Probably shortly after you did. I asked him about Shayla's drowning. He didn't tell me anything we didn't already know."

"Did you ask him about my father?"

He met her gaze. "I did, and he quickly shut me down. He said I should be careful I didn't do anything to hurt you or your aunt."

"That's not exactly saying he's sure my father is completely innocent."

"I know. It's possible he didn't want to bring your dad into it, but then again I don't think he would have looked the other way if he felt a crime had occurred. He's loyal to your aunt, but he's a good cop."

"Speaking of my father," she said. "My dad showed up at the hospital."

"How was that?"

"Weird. I saw him a year ago for about ten minutes. Before that, we'd gone five years without seeing each other. Anyway, he spoke briefly to Phoebe and then he showed up here. That's what I found to be really strange."

"Why? Maybe he wanted to talk to you."

"He seemed more interested in the boxes than talking to me. In fact, he was going through them when I walked in. He said Evie let him in, but she wasn't here when I got here."

"Are you still thinking he was involved with Shayla?"

"I don't think it. I know it. I asked him, Braden."

"What did he say?"

"At first he denied it. We got into a heated discussion about the divorce, and I don't know what came over me. All the bottled up feelings I had about him just came pouring out. I asked him why he hadn't fought for me, why he'd divorced me as well as my mother."

Braden gave a low whistle. "That was brave."

"Or stupid. He hedged the way he always did, made up rationalizations, but it didn't matter what he said. Because it wasn't really about him, it was about me. I needed to say what I'd always wanted to say."

"I'm impressed," he said with a glint of admiration in his eyes. "It's not easy to confront a parent, especially someone like your dad."

"I'm a little impressed with myself," she admitted. "I didn't know I could really talk to him like an equal until I did it. Anyway, at some point in the discussion I asked him flat out if he'd had an affair with Shayla. He blustered that it wasn't any of my business, but I didn't let him off the hook, and finally he admitted that he'd known her."

"I'm more impressed."

"He insisted they were just friends, but he did say that he'd been at a birthday party for her, and that probably was his lighter that I saw in the photograph. He also asked me for the pictures, but I said I didn't have them, and he seemed very disturbed by that. I told him you have them, and he asked if I could get them back and bring them to breakfast tomorrow."

"You're having breakfast with him?"

She nodded. "It's been a long time since he asked me to do anything with him. I couldn't say no. And it might be a good opportunity to ask him more questions about Shayla."

"I gave the photos to Drew."

"Oh, well, that was probably a good idea."

"I didn't say anything about the lighter possibly belonging to your dad."

It touched her that Braden's first instinct was to protect her. "I appreciate that."

"Drew thinks we're out of our minds by the way."

She smiled. "Some days I think that, too."

"I also checked in with my sister, and you might be interested to know that Daniel Stone rented the house for Shayla or for himself. Who knows? Maybe she was his guest."

"That's interesting," she said.

"Shayla's name was on the rental the year before... so I don't know why that changed."

"I guess we need to talk to Mr. Stone. Shayla would be about the same age as Daniel if she'd lived. It makes more sense that they would have been involved with each other, than that she was involved with Jack. And when you think about it, Daniel is really the only one of our suspects who would be motivated to cover up the past. My dad doesn't have anything to lose by the revelation of an affair. And he could have just asked my aunt to let him in the shop if he wanted to look through the boxes."

"I do think your father is a long shot," Braden agreed. "At least for the break-in and for whatever happened to Shayla. He wasn't in town when she died, and as you say, he didn't need to break into his sister's store. Daniel, on the other hand, could be concerned that his relationship with Shayla might somehow come back to haunt him."

"Like if she was in love with him and killed herself. He might not want anyone to know that." She paused. "If she left a note or a journal or something in the Wellbourne house, maybe Jack hung on to it. Perhaps Daniel or one of his people decided to make sure nothing was suddenly coming to light."

Braden smiled.

"What?" she asked suspiciously.

"You look like a kid at Christmas. Maybe you should change careers and become a detective."

"We're working on finding you a new job, not me."

"We'll see," he said.

Now that they'd finished comparing notes, a silence lengthened between them, turning a little tense and uncomfortable. There was nothing else to focus on besides themselves.

She cleared her throat. "So…"

"So…" Braden echoed.

"Do you want to talk about what happened earlier?"

"No. You?"

"I could let it be for now," she said, not sure she would be able to speak clearly and definitively about what she thought or what she wanted. Her mind was too muddled.

"Then, we'll let it be. What are you doing for dinner?"

"I haven't made any plans."

"I'm meeting my mother and sister at Rocco's."

"Is that place still around? I loved their pizza."

"It's still around. You should come."

"I wouldn't want to intrude."

"Actually, it would probably be good for me if you were there. Then they won't be able to hound me about my life choices. Carey has worked up a plan for me to be a realtor with her."

She smiled as he rolled his eyes. "You need something with a little more action."

"What I need is for people to let me figure it out."

"Hey, my ideas were more creative. And you didn't even let me get to my latest idea that you should be a pilot."

"I was in the Army not the Air Force."

"I know, but you have that cool, calm, *I can get this plane down safely* kind of demeanor."

"Well, thanks for the vote of confidence, but I suspect most passengers would like experience over demeanor. And you cannot come to dinner unless you promise to drop the career talk."

"Are you sure they won't mind if I'm there?"

"They'll be thrilled."

"My coming might raise more questions for you, Braden. People seem to be very interested in the fact that we're working together."

"Whatever they ask about you will be better than the questions I've been getting on Kinley."

"Did they like her?"

"My mom really tried, but she and Kinley didn't click. They're just too different."

"So, you want me to come and be your buffer. I think that's just about the nicest invitation I've ever gotten," she mocked.

He laughed. "I'll let you put vegetables on the pizza," he said, reminding her of the many times he'd made her eat a plain cheese pizza, because he didn't like all the "green stuff".

"Sold," she said, as she grabbed her purse and followed him out the door.

Chapter Eleven

Rocco's Pizza Palace was a landmark in Sand Harbor and had been owned and operated by various members of the Domenici family for almost fifty years. As Braden held open the door to the old-fashioned pizza parlor, Alexa felt like she was stepping back in time, not only because the décor in the restaurant was old, but because this restaurant had been one of her favorites as a kid. She'd eaten here with her own family and also with Braden's.

Braden's mother and sister were at a table in the center of the room, and Alexa had no problem recognizing Kathy Elliott. She was still blonde and petite, with warm brown eyes and a soft smile. Kathy jumped to her feet and enveloped Alexa in a warm hug before she even had a chance to say hello.

"Oh, my goodness, Alexa. I'd recognize you anywhere. It's wonderful to see you again," Kathy said with a broad smile as she stepped back and gave her a long look. "You're beautiful."

She flushed at the compliment. "Thank you. You look good, too. And Carey, wow!" She gave Braden's sister an admiring smile. "You're all grown up. In my mind, you're still ten."

"And you're twelve," Carey said, also giving her a hug.

The women in the Elliott family had always been huggers, a trait that did not extend to Braden.

"You didn't mention you were bringing Alexa," Carey said, giving her big brother a curious look.

"It was a spur of the moment thing," he said, pulling out a chair for Alexa.

"I hope you don't mind," Alexa said as they all sat down.

"No, it's great," Kathy replied. "I was thrilled when Carey said Braden was actually willing to have a meal with us. And I'm even happier now that you're here. I heard about your aunt. It's just terrible what happened to her. How is she doing?"

"Really well. They anticipate a full recovery."

"That's a blessing," Kathy said. "I don't know what Sand Harbor is coming to. We never used to have any crime at all."

"Why don't I get us some drinks?" Braden suggested. "And do you know what kind of pizza you want?"

"Not plain cheese," Carey said with a pointed look in Braden's direction.

"I already promised Alexa she could order vegetables," he retorted. "Although I don't know what's wrong with cheese and tomato sauce."

"It's boring. Just like the vanilla ice cream you insist on eating."

Alexa smiled at the warm teasing conversation between Braden and Carey. The two had always been close, and their relationship had made her wish for a sibling on more than one occasion. "Actually, vanilla ice cream is my favorite, too," she said, deciding to give Braden a little help. "We'll have to get some later."

He grinned back at her. "As long as you don't douse it in hot fudge."

"Killjoy."

"Why don't you get us an extra-large pizza, half veggie, half meat," Carrie suggested. "And some diet soda."

"Because God knows you should save the calories for all that pizza," he said dryly.

"Exactly," his sister replied with a smile.

As Braden left, Carey said, "He seems almost normal tonight."

Kathy nodded, turning to Alexa. "Braden has been keeping to himself a lot since he got out of the service. We've been worried about him. He's been in such a funk. I couldn't talk to him about anything without him snapping my head off."

"It sounds like he's had a rough time," Alexa said. She was very curious to learn more about Braden's past, but she doubted he'd appreciate the fact that they were talking about him.

"Did he tell you he's getting divorced?" Carey asked.

"He mentioned it."

"Did he tell you why?"

"No, and he said he didn't plan to, either," she replied.

"Well, at least Braden has been talking a little," Carey murmured, sitting back in her chair with a thoughtful look. "He rarely speaks about Kinley. I haven't been able to get more than two words out of him. I know that she cheated on him. Did he tell you that?"

"He did mention something about that."

"Maybe he'll tell you more," Carey said. "He needs to talk to someone."

"I don't think it will be me," Alexa replied. "We're practically strangers now."

"It doesn't really seem that way," Kathy said softly. "When the two of you walked in together, it felt so right. I remember thinking when you were both kids that you had a very special connection. Braden looked forward to the summer so much. Once you arrived, I barely saw him. He'd take off on his bike in the morning and not come back until dinner time."

"Those were the good old days," Alexa said. "I don't think I appreciated how good they were at the time. But it was a long time ago. We've lived a lot of years apart. We're different now."

"But you're not married?" Carrie ventured.

She shook her head. "Nope, I'm single."

"Interesting," Carey said, her gaze moving from Alexa to Braden and then back again.

Thankfully, Alexa didn't have to say more as Braden returned to the table with a pitcher of soda and a bottle of beer. As he took his seat, a frown turned down his lips. "Gossiping about me?" he asked suspiciously.

"It's not always about you, Braden," Carey retorted. "We're just getting to know Alexa again. What kind of job do you do?" she added, turning to Alexa.

"I'm an accountant," she said.

"I'll bet you're glad April 15th has passed," Kathy said. "I don't know how you do it, Alexa. I cringe every time I have to go back through my old receipts. Every year I swear I'm going to get more organized, and every year it's the same mess."

"You're not alone, trust me, I've had people bring me receipts in shoe boxes and shopping bags. One guy kept them in a pillow case."

Braden smiled.

"What's so funny?" she asked.

"Just thinking that those shopping bags full of receipts probably seem a little like a treasure hunt to you."

"Sometimes," she admitted. "It can be a challenge to piece together someone's financial history. It's amazing that people who look successful and polished on the outside sometimes have the most chaotic organizational system. I've learned not to pre-judge."

"I feel the same way about the people who come to my real estate office," Carey said. "I've only been a realtor for a year, but I'm still amazed at what people think they can afford based on their actual income. Not that there isn't a lot of wealth in town. Those houses along the beach just keep going up in value." She paused. "You and Braden are trying to hunt down information on the Wellbourne house, right?"

"We're curious about the woman who stayed there the last summer I was in town," Alexa said. "Shayla Cummings."

Kathy started. "Who are you talking about?"

"The woman who drowned," Alexa said. "Braden and I saw a fight between Shayla and someone the night before I left, and then she died under mysterious circumstances, so we're curious."

Kathy shook her head, her lips tightening. "You shouldn't be digging into that old history."

Braden straightened at his mother's tone. "Why not?" he asked.

"That young woman was trouble. The wives in town were worried whenever she came to town. She got a lot of male attention."

"Anyone in particular?" Braden asked.

Kathy shot Alexa a quick look and then turned to her son. "I don't like to spread gossip."

"I already know that my father knew Shayla," Alexa said. "He told me they were friends."

"Yes, she had a lot of friends," Kathy said, a pointed note in her voice.

"You make her sound like a slut, Mom," Carey interjected.

"Well, I don't like to use that word, but she didn't have a good reputation."

"Was she involved with Daniel Stone?" Braden asked. "Carey looked up the rental records for the Wellbourne house, and Daniel Stone's name was on the lease for the month of August."

"Daniel was wild as a young man, as were the Wellbourne boys. They were always having big parties on their parents' yachts. I'm sure they all knew Shayla. And not just the sons, but their fathers, too." Kathy clapped a hand to her mouth. "I can't believe I just said that out loud."

"Well, you did," Braden said quickly. "Was Jack Wellbourne having an affair with Shayla?"

"There were some rumors to that effect," Kathy admitted. "The Wellbournes were always traveling or splitting time between here and their other homes, so no one ever knew where they were. But Jack seemed to be showing up a lot more often that summer to check up on his investments."

"There was a big age gap between Jack and Shayla," Alexa put in.

"Rich, older men don't usually have a problem finding eager, young, beautiful women," Kathy said.

"Did you know Roberta Wellbourne, Mom?" Braden asked.

"Not well," Kathy replied. "She was also younger than Jack, and she was always about money. She used to encourage Jack to raise the rents in town, sometimes driving people out of their businesses. I didn't like her at all. I can't believe she's back now and running Daniel Stone's campaign. She may think she's an asset, because of her past in Sand Harbor, but she's wrong. People around here have long memories, and I almost feel sorry for Daniel that he's aligned himself with her." Kathy paused. "Let's talk about something else."

"In a minute," Braden said.

"He's not going to stop, Mom," Carey interrupted, sipping on her diet coke. "You know how Braden is when he gets that stubborn look in his eyes."

"Thanks for the help, Carey," Braden said.

"Any time."

"What can you tell me about Edwin Hayes and Jack Wellbourne?" Braden asked his mom.

"Why?" Kathy asked with a sigh.

"The police investigation into Shayla's death seemed a little short," he said.

"Braden, I don't want you involved in this. You've had enough trouble in your life, why look for more?" Kathy asked.

"Because of that fight Alexa and I saw. It makes us both curious."

"You, too, Alexa?"

Alexa gave an apologetic shrug. "Sorry, but yes. Maybe it's because I'm revisiting my past that I'm so interested in Shayla. I always thought of her as this cool, beautiful woman in this big, dreamy house, and to learn that she died shortly after I saw her was unsettling, especially since no one seems to know what really happened to her."

"You never told me about a fight, Braden," Kathy said.

"I wasn't paying attention to the news."

"Or to much of anything. You were moping because Alexa was gone," Carey said with a teasing smile.

He shot his sister a dark look. "What do you know about it? You were ten."

"I was old enough to know you had a big crush on her."

Alexa smiled at the warmth that spread across Braden's cheeks.

"We're not talking about that," he said.

"Did you know that Braden wrote a song for you, Alexa?" Carey asked. "He used to play it on his guitar for hours on end."

"Where's that pizza?' Braden muttered, looking toward the counter for a much needed interruption.

Alexa was surprised. "I had no idea. You were just learning the guitar when I left."

"It was stupid. I could barely play," Braden said. "It was just something I made up."

"He was better than he's saying," Carey told her. "In high school he got really good. He played in a band, and half of my friends were in love with him.

"Carey, will you just shut up," Braden ordered.

"What? Am I embarrassing you?" she asked unapologetically. "Every girl would love to have a guy write a song for her."

"It is pretty cool," Alexa said. Braden was avoiding her gaze so she turned to Carey. "I had a mad crush on your brother, too."

"I figured," Carey said with a smile. "And now you two have finally met up again. It's so romantic."

"Alexa is leaving in a few days. She has a life far from here," Braden said sharply. "She always did." He got up from his seat. "I'm going to check on the pizza."

"Now, I've pissed him off," Carey said with a sigh. "I can't say much of anything right these days. I hope you know I was only teasing, Alexa."

"I know," she replied, her gaze following Braden. "It's complicated between us."

"Of course it is," Kathy said. "You're both afraid to ruin what you're just getting back – your friendship."

"I did miss Braden terribly," Alexa admitted.

"And he missed you," Kathy replied, giving her a warm smile. "Whatever he says, don't ever doubt that."

Braden returned with two large pizzas and for the next ten minutes all they did was eat. Then the conversation turned to neutral topics like Carey's latest online dating adventure. Braden let his mom and sister do most of the talking, although he occasionally teased Carey for her pickiness when it came to men.

Alexa enjoyed watching him with his mom and his sister. It reminded her of when she was a kid and she'd hung out with his family. She'd only met his dad once when he was home for a weekend visit. But the rest of the time it had just been Braden, his mom, his sister, and his brother. It was clear how much love there was in the group. And it made her a little sad that she'd missed having this kind of family connection growing up. If she'd had a sibling to ease the burden of her mother's depression, life would have been a little easier.

"So have you tried online dating, Alexa?" Carey asked.

"No, I'd be too afraid."

"As long as you pick a public place, you're probably fine."

"Maybe in Sand Harbor. But San Francisco has a few more crazy people."

"I've always wanted to go to San Francisco," Carey said. "Do you ride the cable cars?"

"Only when I have friends visit me from out of town," she said with a laugh.

"Sometimes this town is a little too small for me, but if I did leave, I'd go somewhere in between, perhaps Portland, where Matt is," Carey said. "I've thought about moving there, but I'm kind of lazy. I have so many friends here, and my mom and now Braden." She looked at her brother. "It is nice to have you living here again."

"I don't know that I'll be staying," he said.

Alexa saw the dismay flash in Carey and Kathy's eyes.

"You're thinking of leaving?" Kathy asked.

"It's an option."

"Because of Kinley. You don't want to run into her all the time," Carey said with disappointment.

"Well, that's one reason."

"Kinley will probably leave before you do," Carey said. "I ran into her sister the other day, and she said Kinley is thinking of moving to L.A."

Braden shrugged. "I don't know her plans – or mine, for that matter."

"Well, you don't need to decide tonight," Kathy said quietly. "Whatever you want to do, we'll support you."

"Thanks."

"So does anyone want to see a movie tonight?" Carey asked, obviously sensing the need for a change in subject.

"I'll go with you," Kathy said.

"Great. Anyone else?"

"I'll pass," Braden said.

"I have some more work to do at the antique shop," Alexa said.

"I'll walk you back," Braden offered. "Are you done?"

"Yes, thank you so much for dinner." She set down her napkin and stood up. "It was really nice to see both of you."

"Hopefully we'll see you again soon," Kathy said, giving her another hug.

Carrie also gave her a hug goodbye, and then Alexa walked outside with Braden.

The air was cool, and she drew her sweater more closely about her body as they started to walk the three blocks to the antique shop. "Do you think they're talking about us now?" she asked.

"Not a doubt in my mind," he said with a sigh.

"Does it bother you?"

"I'm used to my sister and mother being interested in every area of my life. There aren't a lot of boundaries in my family. Matt went to Portland to get a little independence from the female members of the family. I think he had the right idea.

"I like your family. You're lucky to have each other. I hope you realize that."

"I do."

As she gave a little shiver, he put an arm around her shoulders. "You're cold," he said, as if he needed to give himself a reason to touch her.

She didn't care what his reason was, she just like being closer to him. "This is better. What did you think of your mom's suggestion that Shayla was involved with Jack Wellbourne?"

"We certainly have a growing list of viable candidates for people who might have been fighting with Shayla that night. The odd thing is that most of them are back in town – your father, Daniel Stone, Roberta Wellbourne…"

"But my father wasn't here during the robbery, and he wouldn't have assaulted his own sister."

"Maybe he didn't assault her. Drew seemed to think that your aunt might have fallen and hit her head on the counter."

"Well, he wouldn't have left her on the floor bleeding," she retorted. "He's not that horrible of a person."

"Sorry. You're right. It couldn't have been him."

Now that she didn't have to defend her father to Braden, she felt the need to defend him to herself. "But it is odd that he wasn't reachable by phone the day after the accident and then he showed up here and wanted to help me in the antique shop. None of that made sense to me. He was very interested in those boxes. But he wouldn't hurt his sister. Phoebe practically raised him and my Uncle Stan. They adore her. My father is selfish, but he's not violent. He might have yelled at my mother, but he never physically abused her, not that the mental abuse wasn't bad." She let out a sigh. "I'm rambling. Stop me."

"Let's just walk," he said. "It's a nice night."

"It is," she said.

All the shops on this block were closed, so it was very quiet – probably too quiet for a lot of people, but she was beginning to remember how much she'd liked life in a small town.

"I feel like San Francisco is really far away right now," she said a few minutes later.

"Do you miss your city by the bay?"

"It's a beautiful place: the water, the bridges, the steep hills and magnificent skyscrapers. Oh, and the food is amazing. You can find something from every country in the world, and it's good."

"How did you end up there?"

"A girlfriend from college needed a roommate. I was tired of the snow in Virginia, so I found a job out there. I work on the forty-second floor. Sometimes, the elevator ride makes me dizzy."

"Have you been through an earthquake yet?"

"A small one. The building swayed like a ballet dancer. I guess that was what it was supposed to do."

"Do you live that high up as well?"

"No, I'm on the second floor of a very small apartment building in Russian Hill."

"Russian Hill. That sounds cool."

"You should come and see me," she said.

"It's your life, not mine."

She stopped walking and turned to face him. "Braden – I don't mean to be harsh, but you don't really have a life right now. You could start over anywhere you wanted."

His gaze was steady. "And you think I should start over in San Francisco?"

Her pulse jumped. "I don't know. But I think you should stop talking in absolutes – for either of us," she added. "My life is just my life. I can live it anywhere. I can be happy in a lot of places. I feel like you use the fact that I have an address somewhere else against me."

"I don't think I'm doing that."

"You just told your mother and sister that I wasn't staying, and that's why we weren't getting involved."

"Well, you aren't staying, are you?"

She drew in a breath. "I don't know what I'm doing, but I don't want you to make my decisions for me. Just like you don't want me to pick a career for you. So let me pick my address."

"Understood," he said.

"Okay, good. Now, there's something else."

"What's that?"

She gave him a smile. "I was wondering about that song you wrote for me."

He groaned. "My sister has a big mouth, and I had a feeling you weren't going to forget that."

"How did the song go?"

"I don't remember."

"Liar. I bet you remember every word."

"I might be able to pull it out of my subconscious, but only if I had my guitar, and I don't."

"I remember when you took your first lesson. You thought you might be a rock star if you decided not to go into the Army."

"*You* decided I should be a rock star," he corrected. "You said rock stars were hot."

"They are hot," she said with a laugh. "As Carey said, what girl doesn't like a guy with a guitar singing his heart out to her?"

"It might have been a better career path."

The somberness of his words took her smile away. "Did you like being a soldier, Braden? I know you chose it because you wanted to be like your dad. But did you like it?"

He gave her a thoughtful look. "No one ever asked me that."

"Well, did you?"

"I did like it. I felt like I had a purpose, and I learned a lot. It was tough at times, but the Army made me better. Unfortunately, there's a fine line between pushing yourself to the limit and breaking."

"Are you talking about your injuries?"

"No, not exactly."

She frowned, sensing she was getting close to something important. "Can you tell me more?" she asked gently.

He let out a sigh. "I don't even know if I can explain it."

She waited, letting him work it out.

"I was proud to serve my country," he said finally. "It was an honor to fight alongside some of the best men I've ever met in my life." He took a breath. "All I ever wanted to be was a man my father would be proud of. That's what drove every decision

I made. I'd ask myself the question -- what would my dad do? He was such a huge influence in my life. However, the longer I served, the more I realized that I needed to start living for myself. And I didn't want to be a career soldier. I didn't want to live that life forever."

"I don't think there's any shame in deciding to move on."

"That wasn't the shameful part." He gazed down at her, his face filled with shadows from the moonlight. "My unit got ambushed. Everyone thinks I got hurt killing the enemy, but that's not what happened."

"What did happen?"

He hesitated another moment, the pulse in his jaw beating fast and furiously. "I don't know if I can say it."

"You can," she encouraged. "Whatever it is. Just tell me."

"We'd been through a series of fire fights in the last month. Everyone's nerves were on edge. We were patrolling a village and supposedly keeping the peace but then some guys started throwing rocks. It wasn't a big deal, I didn't think, but..." His voice trailed away for a long moment, and then he said, "Pete snapped. He got so pissed off, he pulled out his weapon, and he fired at those young, stupid men." Braden bit down on his lip. "I yelled at him to stop, and then he turned on me. His eyes were glazed. He wasn't there. I could see something inside of him was gone."

"He shot you?" she breathed.

"Yeah, and I shot back. Because I thought he was going to kill everyone, not just me."

"Oh, Braden." She put her hand on his arm, feeling the tension in his body. "What happened to him?"

"He survived. I didn't kill him, if that's what you're asking. But he ended up in a psych ward somewhere. He was pushed too far, and he broke."

"What about the villagers that he shot at?"

"There were injuries, thankfully no fatalities. We were lucky that his actions didn't start a full-fledged assault on our unit. As it was, I'm sure it took them weeks to regain trust." He paused. "I knew I had to get out. I didn't want to end up like Pete."

"You never would have," she said with confidence.

"I'm sure he didn't think he'd crack like that, either. I should have seen that he was hurting. I was his closest friend. I was too caught up in myself. I didn't see what was right in front of me. Those deaths would have been on my head."

She saw the pain and guilt in his eyes. "That's why you don't think you're a hero. But you are, Braden. You saved lives that day. And if someone had died, it wouldn't have been because of you. Pete was responsible for his actions."

"He wasn't Pete anymore. He was a stranger."

"I'm sorry for what happened to him. But you're not to blame. You can't know what's going on inside someone's head."

"I was his friend," he said helplessly.

"I'm sure you were a good friend, but everyone has secrets, Braden. Everyone. And you are a hero to me." Her eyes blurred with unexpected tears. "I'm even more convinced of that now, not less."

His jaw tightened. "Alexa –"

"No, don't try to convince me otherwise."

"You're not seeing me for who I am."

"I see you very clearly. You're the only one who's confused." She took a breath. "And whatever you do from here on out, you should do for yourself. I know that following in your dad's footsteps was important to you, but you're right, you have to live your life for yourself. If your dad were still alive, he'd be the first person to tell you that."

"I don't know about that. He loved the Army."

"He loved you more. You used to read me his letters, remember? He was such a good writer, so great at expressing himself, at encouraging you and supporting you and telling you how much he loved you. There's no doubt in my mind that he only wanted the best for you." She paused, trying to lighten the intense mood. "Maybe you got your song-writing talent from him."

Braden let out a breath. "I don't think he would want to take credit for that."

"I still want to hear my song."

"Maybe one of these days."

"Hey, perhaps it's not too late to be a rock star," she said. "That could be your new job."

His lips curved into a smile. "You don't quit."

"It's just an idea."

"Another bad one. What about you, Alexa? You explained the accounting gig to me, but is it really everything you want?"

"It's okay," she said, wishing she could tell him it was truly her passion. "How many people love their job?"

"Maybe a better question is why waste time doing something you don't love?"

"Because I like to eat."

He gave her a look of disbelief. "You could make money doing a lot of things. And sometimes you have to feed your soul, too."

A little shiver ran down her spine. "That was poetic."

"I have my moments. I want to show you something," he said abruptly.

"What?" she asked in surprise.

He grabbed her hand.

"Where are we going?" she asked as she hurried along next to him.

"You'll see. Trust me, you're going to love it."

Chapter Twelve

Alexa was breathless by the time they turned the corner. Braden stopped abruptly in front of a boutique. On display were beautiful pieces of colorful glass, illuminated by small lights. The sign on the building read *The Glass House.*

"What's this?" she asked, mesmerized by the shimmering colors of the glass figures. There were doves and swans, owls and hawks, and a glass tree with thin, delicate branches. Moving her gaze to another display case, she saw several necklaces lying against black velvet.

"The jewelry is made out of sea glass," Braden said. "The other pieces are hand-blown, I believe."

Her breath caught in her throat. She felt both happy and incredibly sad at the same time. This was her dream. This was what she had always wanted to do. But someone else had actually done it. "Who is the glassmaker?"

"Mary Mulligan."

She shook her head at the unfamiliar name. "I don't think I know her."

"You used to call her the bird lady."

She looked at him in surprise. "The woman who used to feed the birds on the beach every afternoon?"

"And collect glass. You were always afraid she was going to beat you to the best pieces."

"Obviously, she did."

"Her daughter helped her open the shop a few

years ago. She'd apparently been making the figures for years in her garage, but it was just a hobby. Half the time she'd just give away her pieces."

"They're beautiful," she said, gazing back at the glass. A wave of emotion hit her again. She felt like she could see her life in the glass, the innocent dreams of a young girl that had never come to fruition.

"I didn't mean to make you sad," Braden said.

She blinked back a shocking tear. "No, my eyes are just watering. It must be the breeze."

"There's no wind, Alexa." He turned her to face him, putting his hands on her shoulders. "What's wrong?"

"It's weird seeing my dream come true, only I didn't do it."

"You still could. It took Mary forty years to open her shop."

"I wonder if she makes any money. If you calculate the rent and the number of pieces, and how much she would have to sell them for, it's doubtful that she's turning a profit."

He smiled. "Stop. We're not being practical tonight. This is just for you to enjoy."

She drew in a deep breath, glanced back at the glass and said, "I do like it, Braden. Thank you for showing it to me."

"Well, you're not the only one who gets to psychoanalyze."

"That's fair. You know, I don't have any friends from my childhood, except for you. Everyone I know now I met as an adult, or at least in college. But I don't spend time with anyone who knew me before my family fell apart."

"So you can get away without revealing too much of yourself."

"Yes. I'm just Alexa the accountant to them. They don't question why I don't make necklaces out of sea glass. In fact, they'd probably think I was nuts if I mentioned I wanted to do that."

"Then it's good you came back here. Maybe you needed someone to question your choices."

"Yeah, it's great," she said dryly. "Now I'll go home and start thinking that my job really sucks. Before, I was living in relatively happy denial."

He grinned. "The good thing about jobs is that you can change them. You're not what you do, Alexa."

She punched him on the arm. "Look who's talking. You can't stop thinking of yourself as a soldier."

"I'm trying."

"Maybe we should find a guitar store."

"I think we've done enough soul searching for one night. Do you really want to go back to the antique shop? It's getting late. I don't want to leave you there alone."

"You're right. I'm tired anyway. I'll go back to the inn."

He nodded. "Good plan.   I'll walk you over there."

"I'm fine on my own."

"I'm going with you. Don't argue."

Braden had always had protective instincts. Even as a twelve-year-old, he'd watched out for her. She'd always felt safe with him.

But right now safety was the last thing on her mind. Reckless thoughts were flashing through her head. She felt like a teenager wondering if her date was going to kiss her goodnight and if she was going to kiss him back.

By the time they reached the front door, she was

no closer to a conclusion, but she was definitely wound up.

Braden seemed tense again, too. They looked at each other a minute too long.

"Well, good-night," she said, finally finding her voice. "I had fun. It was nice to spend time with your family."

His jaw tightened, and he looked almost angry when he said, "Damn, Alexa. I want to kiss you again."

A tingle shot down her spine. "Don't sound so happy about it."

He shook his head, putting his hands in his pockets in a decisive gesture. "I'm not going to, but I want to."

She didn't like that he wasn't giving her a say in the matter. "It's not all up to you," she said. And before he could reply, she had breached the gap between them, pressed her hands against his chest and kissed him on the mouth.

His lips parted with surprise, and she took advantage, sliding her tongue into his mouth, angling her head so she could deepen the kiss. She wanted to break down the wall he'd just put back up between them. It bothered her that he would pull down his guard, let her get close, and then shove her away again.

After a momentary resistance, Braden put his hands on her waist and pulled her up against his chest. And just like that he took charge of the kiss. It didn't matter. She didn't need the control. *She needed him.*

The thought rattled her so badly she broke away. She didn't want to *need* any man. It made her vulnerable.

"Alexa?" Braden questioned, his gaze raking her

face.

She put a hand to her lips, still feeling the branding heat of his mouth. "I – Goodnight," she said, and dashed into the inn.

For a moment she thought he might follow, that the door would open behind her while she was waiting for the elevator. But aside from the clerk at the main desk giving her a curious look, she was alone.

She went upstairs to her room. Once inside, she crossed to the window and looked out at the front sidewalk. Braden was gone.

Well, why would he hang around? She'd run away from him.

Just like he'd run away from her earlier that day.

One of these days they were both going to have to stick around and face the music.

* * *

Alexa was relieved when the sun finally streamed through the curtains early Friday morning. She hadn't been able to sleep all night, tossing and turning, thinking about Braden, wondering if she should stay in Sand Harbor or if she should go home before she made some really stupid decision. Braden was making her question everything about her life, her job, where she lived, and her resolve not to get emotionally involved with anyone who might hurt her.

Braden could definitely hurt her, but she hadn't felt so attracted to a man in a very long time. She almost ached with wanting to see him, to touch him, to make love to him. And it wasn't just the physical attraction, she felt emotionally connected to him. That's what scared her the most. No one had ever really touched her core. Braden hadn't gotten there yet, but he was damn close. She wanted him, but she didn't want him to have power over her. She didn't know how to have him and not need him. She didn't want to end up like her mother.

But it wasn't just herself that she needed to consider. Braden was at a vulnerable time in his life as well. His marriage was finished. His career was over. He was reeling from what had happened to his friend, how they'd gone from brothers to enemies in one snap of a second.

As much as she wanted to be the one to pick him up, to make it all better, she had to protect herself, too. And speaking of protecting herself, she had to stop thinking about Braden and concentrate on what was coming next – meeting her father.

She finished dressing, and then left the inn to go to Hannah's Bagel House. She arrived before her dad, so she ordered a selection of bagels, grabbed some coffee, and took a seat at a nearby table. The Bagel House was on the wharf, and it was fun watching the boats sailing out of the harbor. Being in Sand Harbor made her feel like she was on vacation. Her father had actually disliked the town for the very same reason. He'd always complained that he couldn't get any work done in such a lazy place, that he needed the pace and the energy of a big city.

She wasn't exactly sure where she fell on the issue. She'd only ever worked in a big city, so she didn't know what the distractions would be in a small town. And she didn't really know where her place was. Like Braden, she'd set the goals for her life when she was a teenager. While he'd based a lot of his decisions on what his father would do, she'd made most of her decisions based on a desire not to end up like her mother. But as she'd told Braden last night, he needed to live his life. Maybe she needed to take her own advice.

While she was waiting for her bagels to be toasted, she picked up a local paper that someone had discarded. On the front page was a picture of Daniel Stone. He was shaking hands with the President of the United States. The accompanying article talked about his fundraiser and his senate campaign.

Daniel was a good-looking man, a power player, she thought. There was a hint of ruthlessness about his eyes. He was ambitious. Had he always been that way? Had there been a time in his life when a young woman's tragic death might have proved a problem to him? Just from looking at his picture, he seemed like someone who might cover up a crime. Or maybe she was just taking a cynical view.

The door opened, and her father came in with a chilling breeze. She hoped that wasn't a sign of bad things to come. She set down her paper and steeled herself for whatever was coming. For some reason, she didn't think it would be good.

He gave her a nod and walked over to join her. He was dressed in a suit, which was the way she always pictured him in her mind.

"I ordered some bagels," she said, as he pulled out the chair across from her. "They should be ready in a second. I didn't know your favorite, so I ordered a variety."

Her father gave her a regretful smile. "I'm afraid I can't stay. I had to change my flight. Work came up. I just wanted to say goodbye."

A crushing wave of disappointment hit her. She felt like a little girl again. She flashed back on the first year of the divorce when he'd promised to come by and see her and something had always come up. But she wasn't a kid any more. She could handle this.

"Okay," she said, refusing to add, *it's fine,* because she'd let him off the hook far too many times. "Are you going to say good-bye to Aunt Phoebe?"

"I already did."

"Good."

"You grew up to be a beautiful woman, Alexa. Smart and talented, too. I'm proud of you."

She didn't want to care about his compliments. He was just trying to make her feel better for ditching her. "You don't have to flatter me. It doesn't change anything."

"I'm just speaking the truth. I know I let you down many, many times."

"Including today," she pointed out.

"I know. I doubt I can ever make up for any of it."

"I doubt you'll ever try," she said.

"You've learned how to hit hard."

"I learned from the best," she said. "And I'm not talking about my mother; I'm talking about you."

He didn't look pleased with her comment. "I do want to try, Alexa. I'd like to have you come down to L.A. and spend the weekend with us. The kids would like to get to know you better. You're their sister."

She sighed. "You never ever follow up on these invitations. I'd rather you just didn't offer them."

"I mean it this time. I love you, Alexa. Maybe not the way you want me to, but I do."

He paused, probably waiting for her to say she loved him, too, but she'd already told him that yesterday and he was running out on breakfast. What more did she have to give?

"You asked about Shayla yesterday," he continued. "I didn't sleep with her. And I don't know how she died. But I do know that she kept a journal.

She wrote in it all the time. She said one day she was going to write her memoir. I teased her that she'd need a dozen more journals for that; she was too young to think about that. When I heard that she had drowned, I didn't know what to think."

"Did you think she killed herself?" Alexa asked.

"Unfortunately, I suspected just that. She had told me she was in love with someone who was unavailable. Apparently, she'd gotten pregnant and he'd asked her to get an abortion. She'd agreed, because she wasn't ready to have a baby, and because she was afraid that she would lose him if she didn't. But she was haunted by what she'd done. She used to go out on the deck and stare into the sea and wonder about her choices."

"I saw her on that deck so many times," Alexa murmured. "She was this beautiful romantic figure. But it doesn't sound like she was happy at all."

"The first summer she came to Sand Harbor, she was happy, but things changed the second time around."

"Why did you decide to tell me this?" she asked curiously.

"Because of what you said -- that you think the break-in and Shayla's death are connected. You need to look for that journal."

"I haven't seen it. I've been through all the boxes."

"Then maybe someone got there before you."

"If you had to pick between Jack Wellbourne and Daniel Stone, who would you say might have been her lover?"

Her dad thought for a long moment. "It could have been either one. Or it could have been someone else. She was a flame and men danced around her."

"What was it about her that made her so

attractive? Was it just her beauty?"

"She had a charm, a way of looking at a man that made him feel special."

It stung to hear her father talk about another woman like that. Although, she couldn't say she was at all surprised. "You didn't feel special with Mom?"

"I felt trapped. Her need for me was too much. She clung to me."

"How can you say that when you were the one who was always leaving?" she asked in amazement.

"That's why I was always leaving. When I was with her, she was all over me. She couldn't sit across the room. She couldn't stop talking. She couldn't just listen, just be. It was exhausting."

There was a part of her that understood his frustration, because her mother had clung to her, too.

He stood up as the bagels were delivered to the table. "I should go."

"Do you want to take one for the road?"

"No, I'm good." He offered her a tentative smile. "Can I offer a word of advice?"

"I guess," she said, feeling a bit wary by the offer.

"Don't get so caught up in the past, you forget to enjoy your present. I want you to be happy, Alexa. Find your passion and live it. Love someone who makes you better, someone who builds you up, because there are enough people in this world who will try to tear you down. And don't ever be like me. I want more for you than that."

"I want more for me than that, too."

She watched him walk away with mixed feelings. They'd had a small breakthrough. Would it last? Who knew?

* * *

After finishing her bagels and coffee, Alexa headed down the street. It was nice that everything was so close. She didn't have to take her car; she could just walk and enjoy the spring weather. She meant to go straight to the antique shop, but when she reached the corner, she impulsively changed directions. The Glass House was just around the corner, and she wanted to take a look inside.

The front door was open, and there was a woman setting out a beautiful glass hawk on one of the display shelves. She looked familiar with her frizzy gray hair, leggings and long sweater. This was the woman she'd called the bird lady. Apparently, she'd tried to capture her love of birds in her glass.

"Can I help you?" the woman asked, giving her a friendly smile. She had warm blue eyes and a slight Irish lilt to her voice.

"I'm just looking around. You have beautiful pieces."

"Thank you."

"I'm Alexa Parker. My aunt owns the antique shop, Yesterday Once More."

"I know Phoebe. Such a dreadful thing that happened to her," the woman said. "I'm Mary Mulligan. It's lovely to meet you."

"You, too. I used to see you on the beach in the summers when I came to visit my aunt. You were always feeding the birds and collecting sea glass."

Mary smiled. "I still go out there every Sunday. I try to capture the beauty of the birds in my glass, but I'm not sure I come that close." She turned a critical eye on her latest piece.

"It's beautiful," Alexa said. "You've captured the grace and power perfectly. I love it."

"Would you like to have it?"

"How much is it?"

"Whatever you can afford," Mary said.

"I wouldn't want to shortchange you."

"I'm sure you won't."

"You're very trusting," she said, pulling out her wallet. "Why don't I give you my credit card and you can charge me what's fair."

Mary took her card and moved to the counter. "How about twenty dollars?"

"I think that's too cheap."

"You sound just like my daughter," Mary said with a sigh. "Janet keeps telling me that I need to charge more to keep up with the rising rent. I wouldn't mind just going back to selling the glass out of my garage or at the local art fair. This business stuff is just not me."

"You could hire someone to help you."

"I wanted Janet to do it, but she decided to be a lawyer instead. I don't know how I raised a kid who would want to wear a suit and study the law," she said with a bewildered smile. "Janet takes after my late husband. He was a businessman, a rule follower, except when it came to me. He learned early on that if we were going to be together, he was going to have loosen up." She handed Alexa the charge slip to sign. "Sadly, he passed on a few years back. That's when Janet decided I should open up the shop and keep myself busy. I was quite happy in my workshop in the garage, but she wanted me to spend more time around people and less time around birds and glass."

Alexa didn't really know what to say, not that Mary seemed to need an answer.

"Is it hard to make the glass pieces?" she asked when Mary finally took a breath.

"It's a little tricky, but anyone can learn. My mother taught me the art when I was a teenager. I wish Janet had been interested, but she didn't like it at all."

"I always wanted to make glass," Alexa admitted. "I used to collect sea glass when I'd come here, and I imagined making a necklace like that one," she said, tipping her head to the one on display.

"Well, instead of imagining, you should do it."

"You make it sound so simple. It's too late for me to learn."

"It's never too late."

"I'm really busy with my job."

"So what do you do that keeps you so busy?" Mrs. Mulligan asked as she carefully put the glass hawk in bubble wrap.

"I'm an accountant."

"Another nine-to-fiver."

"Sometimes it's more like nine to nine," she said, "especially during tax season."

"Well, I've learned over many years that it's important to make time to do the things you love. Isn't that why we're on this earth? We're supposed to enjoy the experience. You should smell the roses or make glass," she added with a smile.

"You're probably right."

In recent months she had begun to realize how isolating her work schedule was. Forget about a serious relationship, she barely had time for friends. But she'd tell herself it would get better after tax season. Unfortunately, there was always something else to do and a new deadline approaching. Maybe she'd just used work as a reason not to date. It was easier to concentrate on business than to worry about hooking up with someone.

"So how long are you in town?" Mary asked.

"I'm not sure. I'm definitely staying until my aunt is home and back on her feet."

"Well, if you have time off, then you should come to my house and I'll show you how to make glass."

"Really?"

"I'd love it. It's not often I meet someone who is interested in the whole process and not just the end piece. It would be a pleasure."

"I'd love to do that."

Mary wrote down her phone number and address on a piece of paper. "The store is closed on Sunday, so come by the house then, if that works for you."

"That should be good," she said.

"If you go out to the beach and find some sea glass beforehand, bring it with you. We'll make something special." She handed Alexa her purchase. "I hope you enjoy this."

"I know I will."

Alexa walked outside and paused on the sidewalk, torn between going to the antique store and heading down to the beach to collect some glass. It was almost as if she was fighting two sides of herself, the little girl who'd been caught up in the magic of the glass that washed up on the beach and the adult who didn't believe in magic anymore.

Another long minute sent her heading in the right direction, she hoped.

Chapter Thirteen

Just after eleven o'clock Friday morning, Braden climbed the steps to the house he'd shared very briefly with Kinley. He paused on the porch, feeling both uncomfortable and oddly detached. He hadn't spent much time in this house. Kinley had bought it when he was overseas, so it didn't really feel like home. He didn't recognize the planters filled with flowers or the wicker swing in the corner. He didn't even recognize the welcome mat. This was Kinley's house, not his. It always had been.

He rang the bell. He still had a key, but it felt wrong to use it now.

Kinley opened the door a moment later. She wore yoga pants and a tight purple top. She'd been working out a lot in recent years, her intense exercise focus becoming another barrier between them.

There was wariness in her eyes, and she didn't invite him in. "What are you doing here, Braden?"

"I need to get a few things," he said.

"I thought you said there wasn't anything or anyone in this house you wanted," she replied, throwing his words back at him.

"I was wrong," he said simply.

Surprise spread across her face. "You were wrong?" she echoed.

He nodded. "About a lot of things. There's no need to rehash all our problems. It's over for both of us. It was finished long before we both said it out loud. I don't respect some of the things you did, but I don't need to be your enemy." As he let go of the anger, he felt lighter. Alexa had told him his wounds were festering, and she was right. He'd been holding everything in, and all he'd been doing was hurting himself.

Kinley frowned, as if she didn't quite know what to make of his attitude. Maybe it was easier for her to handle his animosity than any gesture of kindness and regret.

"I shouldn't have told you about the affair when you were in the hospital," she said finally. "I do regret that, Braden. It just came out. You scared me. When I saw you in the bed with all those bandages, you looked so broken. I barely recognized you. I didn't want to be with a soldier anymore."

"I told you I was going to leave the Army."

"It was too late, Braden."

"I wish you would have told me you wanted out before you cheated."

"I told you why I didn't tell you. I didn't want you to be distracted while you were in danger." She drew in a breath and then let it out. "I'm not proud of what I did. I thought our lives were going to be so different than what they turned out to be. I didn't know I was going to be so lonely. I didn't understand that I'd be giving up a lot to move around with you. And even when you were home, you shut down. You couldn't talk to me. You were sealed up like a vault, and I had no idea how to get in."

She was probably right about that, but she hadn't tried all that hard to understand what he was going through. "I did try to tell you about Pete."

Her lips tightened. "I don't want to talk about that. It's too sad. And I'm afraid if you tell me too much, I'll blurt it out to someone that shouldn't know. I still see some of Pete's friends around town, and no one knows the whole story but you. That's the way you wanted it."

"We don't need to talk about Pete. Can I come in?" he asked.

She hesitated, flinging a quick look over her shoulder. "I'm not alone."

He stiffened, waiting for the anger to come back, but he felt remarkably indifferent to the fact that there was another guy in his house, probably in his bed. They really were done. "Well, I need my guitar," he said.

"Your guitar?" she repeated. "You haven't played that thing since before we married."

"It's in the back closet, or at least it was when I last saw it."

"That's what you came here for – your guitar?" she asked in amazement.

"Yeah," he said. It wasn't just the guitar he was reclaiming it was a part of himself that he'd lost.

"Okay. I'll get it," she said with a shrug. "Can you wait out here? I don't want it to be awkward."

"Yes, God knows, we don't want it to be awkward," he said with a touch of sarcasm.

As Kinley went back inside the house, he walked to the edge of the porch and looked down the street. He doubted he'd ever come back here again, but he no longer felt like he had to avoid this part of town. He needed to move on. He wasn't tied to the Army anymore. He wasn't tied to Kinley. He'd cut all the strings. Now, he just had to figure out how to get started on the rest of his life.

"Here it is," Kinley said, returning a moment later.

"Thanks." He took the case out of her hands.

"What are you going do now, Braden?" she asked curiously.

"Right now, I'm going to see if I remember how to play a few chords."

"I'm talking about your life." She paused, sending him a plea for understanding. "I don't want you to hate me, and I do want you to be happy. You deserve that after everything you've been through."

"I intend to be happy," he said.

"Are you with that woman I saw yesterday?"

"Alexa? No. We're just ... I don't know what we are."

"She's the girl from your past. The one you had a huge crush on. When you told me about her years ago, your voice changed like she was someone special. I always wondered about her."

He couldn't remember exactly what he'd told Kinley about Alexa, but it didn't matter. "She's from my past, yes. I'm not sure yet if she's going to be part of my future."

* * *

Alexa hit the waterfront just as the local restaurants were opening their doors for lunch. There was also a buzzing atmosphere around town as the community prepared for the Daniel Stone fundraiser the next day. Volunteers were on various corners, handing out flyers, and discussing politics, and men and women in conservative business attire stood out in the touristy crowd. She didn't know who they were -- political operatives, security? It was impossible to tell.

She was looking forward to meeting the would-be senator and also his entourage. Her father's remarks about a journal had been tantalizing, but she'd found no such item in any of the boxes at the shop. So either someone had found it before her, or it was still hidden away somewhere. But that was all for later. Right now she had a more personal mission in mind. She was going to find some sea glass.

She took the same path to the beach as she'd done the day before, but once she hit the sand, she kicked off her shoes and let herself enjoy the sensation of the warm grains between her toes. Her last trip to the beach had been filled with purpose, to get to the Wellbourne house. Now she just wanted to enjoy herself.

She wandered down to the water. The tide appeared to be out, which gave her plenty of beach to graze. It still amazed her that the colored gems called sea glass were the result of the ocean currents spinning ordinary glass that had been dumped into the ocean into frosted, colored shards of sea glass. It was nature's way of turning trash into something beautiful, and that appealed to Alexa on a lot of levels. She was tired of people throwing things away – like her father had done with his first family.

She searched for almost an hour, her path taking her along the water. The wind tossed her hair, until half of it was falling loose from her ponytail. The sun toasted her cheeks, making her feel like she'd just come out of a winter cocoon. Walking through the sand was also great exercise. Her legs began to ache from the exertion of squatting down every few feet to examine piles of pebbles, shells and seaweed, hoping to find some colored gem tucked away.

She found a few very small shards early on that she put into a zipped pouch in her bag. But it was slow going, and she was beginning to think she'd have to go home without anything really significant, when she finally stumbled upon a beautiful frosty, dark green piece that was a couple of inches in diameter. She could definitely do something with this.

The sun was getting high in the sky, and she realized it was almost one o'clock. She'd managed to waste half the day, although she didn't want to think of it as a waste. But it was hard to change the habits she'd acquired the last ten years where every activity was pursued for a specific goal. It had been a long time since she had veered off her path of productivity, and she was enjoying the break. She felt more in touch with herself.

As she made her way back across the beach, a figure near the base of the cliff caught her eye. A guy was sitting on a large boulder strumming a guitar, and her heart skipped a beat when she realized it was Braden.

He hadn't seen her yet, his focus on the instrument in his hands. She studied him for a moment, thinking that the guitar made him even sexier -- if that were possible. She liked his casual look, the faded jeans, the gray T-shirt. She couldn't really picture Braden in a suit like the accountants she worked with. She thought he would feel too constricted, although, he had worn a military uniform for almost eight years. He was probably used to being constricted.

Braden suddenly looked up, and his fingers stilled on the guitar.

She waved and walked across the sand. "I see you found your guitar," she said, taking a seat on a large, flat boulder next to him.

"What are you doing down here?"

She held up the piece of sea glass still in her hand.

He sent her a warm, knowing smile. "Reliving old times?"

"I seem to be doing that a lot. I stopped by *The*

Glass House this morning and talked to Mary Mulligan. In fact, I bought one of her bird pieces.

She pulled the box out of her bag and unwrapped the glass so she could show Braden. "Isn't it perfect?"

The glass shimmered in the sunlight, as if the bird was itching to fly away.

"It's beautiful," Braden agreed.

She carefully wrapped the glass back up and returned it to its soft resting place and slid the box into her bag. "Mary invited me to come to her house on Sunday so I can see how she makes the glass. That's something I've always wanted to do."

"I'm glad you're finally doing it," he said approvingly.

"Now that Aunt Phoebe is getting better, I don't feel as guilty about spending a little time for myself."

"You should never feel guilty about that, Alexa. Life is too short."

"I know." She paused. "Speaking of old dreams – how's the music going?"

"I'm very rusty," he said with a grin. "I had to come out here and play where no one could possibly hear me."

"I'm sure you're not that bad."

"I'm sure you have no idea how bad I am."

"Then play for me, and let me be the judge."

He shrugged, then strummed the strings, producing a nice tone.

"That doesn't sound so bad, Braden. What about my song? Can I hear it?"

"I'm still trying to remember the words," he replied.

"I think you remember. You just don't want to sing it for me."

"It was a stupid song, Alexa."

"I want to hear it, Braden." She glanced around.

There was no one nearby. "Right now it's just us and the birds."

He sighed. "You're so pushy."

"And you're so stubborn. Just give me a few lines."

"Fine, but don't blame me if those birds go squawking and squealing into the water."

She laughed. "I'll risk it. Come on."

He glanced down at his guitar and strummed a few chords, and then he began to sing.

His voice was low and smooth, a beautiful masculine tone. But it was the words that touched her.

"*She's my summer girl. Every time I see her, my heart whirls. Her smile lights up a sky that matches her eyes.*"

She drew in a shaky breath as his voice drifted away.

"I don't remember the rest," he muttered, his fingers still playing a pretty melody.

His song took her back to that sweet, innocent love, her first experience with the emotion. There had been so many possibilities then, so much hope, so much yearning...

Braden finally stopped playing to look at her. There was uncertainty in his eyes and maybe a little fear that he'd revealed too much.

"I really loved the boy who wrote that," she said softly.

"I loved the girl I wrote about."

"Do you think they're still a part of us?"

"No."

"Not even down deep?"

He shrugged. "I can only speak for myself. I suspect you still have that girl inside of you."

"You need to write some more," she said.

Just A Wish Away

"Why?"

"Because you won't know what you really have until it's done."

He stared back at her. "Alexa, don't read too much into the song."

"Stop warning me off, Braden. I'll think what I want to think about it and about us."

"Now, who's being stubborn?"

His teasing tone directed the conversation to a lighter note, and she decided to go along with it. "I have to say your music tastes have changed," she said.

"Do you think so?" he asked absentmindedly as he played with the guitar strings.

"Absolutely." She took out her phone and pulled up her playlist. Smiling to herself, she said, "I remember when you liked these guys." She pushed play, and the music from a boy band that was popular two decades ago blasted out of her phone. She'd found the song the night before when she'd been looking for something new to download. She'd been thinking about Braden and the songs they'd used to listen to, wondering if they'd influenced his musical choices.

A grin spread across Braden's face as he looked at her. "They were your favorite, not mine."

"Oh, I don't think so," she said. "You used to dance around and imitate the lead singer." She jumped to her feet and tried to put on the moves she remembered.

Braden set his guitar aside and said, "Give me that phone."

"No way."

And then he was on his feet, headed her way. She squealed and ran, but of course her legs were no match for Braden's long stride. He tackled her into the sand, grabbing the cell phone out of her hand and shutting off the annoying song.

Her heart was beating fast, her breath ragged, and it all got worse when there was nothing but silence, when she became acutely aware of Braden's body sprawled across hers. He gazed down at her, his eyes darkening, his lips parting.

"Alexa," he muttered.

She wrapped her arms around him and pulled him down to her. She loved his weight on top of her, his mouth crushing hers with a passion that went way beyond the sweet little crush they'd shared. They weren't a boy and a girl anymore but a man and a woman. He kissed her like he was starving, like he couldn't get enough of her, and she felt exactly the same way.

She ran her hands up and down his back, feeling the play of his muscles beneath his shirt. Slipping her hands underneath the material, she heard him groan as her fingers ran down the curve of his spine. Her breasts hardened against his chest. An aching need spread through her, and as his lips left her mouth to slide along her jawline and the curve of her neck, she felt herself sigh with longing.

She wanted so much more than a make-out session on the beach, but she had a feeling getting from here to anywhere else was going to bring reason and logic back into the situation, and their passion was not going to make it off the beach.

So she'd just enjoy the moment, she told herself, putting her hands behind his head, running her fingers through the dark waves of his hair, enjoying every touch of his mouth on hers.

And then a barking dog, a splatter of sand from some flying paws, acted like a dose of cold water.

Braden rolled off of her and let out a breath. She

sat up, brushing sand off her arms and out of her hair. Wordlessly, Braden tossed her back the cell phone.

"Thanks," she said.

"This isn't working," Braden said.

"It seemed like it was working pretty well."

"Do you know what you want, Alexa?"

She hesitated, sensing the question could be answered on many different levels. "I know that one day I want to finish the kiss we keep starting."

"And then what?"

"I don't know, Braden. I can't predict the future."

"I can predict part of it. One or both of us gets hurt," he said flatly.

She didn't want to think that's what would happen, but she'd become cynical, too. "You're probably right, but I've been playing it safe for a long time. Maybe it's time I took a chance."

He shook his head, his jaw tight. "I don't know."

She didn't care for his answer.

"Well, when you do know, get back to me," she said rather sharply, as she got to her feet.

"You can't put this all on me," he protested.

"You want it all on you," she said. "You want to be in charge. You want to kiss me when you want to, and stop when you're scared."

"You're the one who stopped last night," he reminded her.

He was right. Her need for him had scared her. "You're right. You make me feel things that are terrifying to me. I saw what happened to my mother when she loved my dad."

"We would never repeat your parents' mistakes."

"No, but we would probably make enough of our own."

"So you don't know what you want," he said.

"I guess I don't. I know this -- we've always had bad timing," she said. "One of us was ready to move forward, and the other one wasn't. I don't know if that still holds true. But at some point, we're going to have to either jump at the same time, or close the door on this forever. This in-between thing is not working for me. In fact, it's making me a little crazy."

"Me, too," he muttered, running a hand through his hair. "I don't want to hurt you, Alexa."

"Then don't."

"I can't decide right now."

"You don't have to." She brushed the sand off of her jeans. "I should go anyway."

"Where are you off to?"

"The antique shop." She paused, smiling a little as she added, "Every time I see the name on the window, Yesterday Once More, I think how very apropos that is to this whole situation. Every day that I'm here feels like it's tied to yesterday."

He nodded. "Yeah, we've been visiting the past a lot."

"Anyway, I want to look through the books that came in with the Wellbourne boxes. My dad told me earlier that Shayla kept a journal. I don't think I saw one when I was unpacking, but maybe it was stuck inside another book."

"Your dad told you that?" he asked in surprise. "You saw him again?"

"Right before he bailed on breakfast."

He frowned. "Seriously? He did that to you? I know he's your father, but he's an ass."

"Yeah, but I'm used to it."

"You shouldn't have to be used to it."

"Well, he did give me a little information before he left. He said Shayla was in love with someone who made her get an abortion. His guess was that it could have been either Jack Wellbourne or Daniel Stone. Shayla told him that the man was unavailable."

"That sounds more like Jack." He paused. "Unless your dad is deliberately trying to steer you away from his involvement."

"It's no wonder I have trust issues when it comes to men," she muttered.

"I hope you don't have that issue with me," Braden said, meeting her gaze. "Because whatever happens between us, you can always trust me not to lie to you, Alexa."

She was touched by his words. "It goes both ways, you know."

He nodded and smiled. "I feel like we should pinky swear now."

She laughed. "Why don't we just seal it with a kiss? One very, short, non-threatening kiss." She went on tiptoe to touch her lips to his, a soft, gentle promise of a kiss, that reminded her very much of the first one they'd ever shared. "I'll see you later."

Chapter Fourteen

One very short, non-threatening kiss, but it still lingered on his lips, as Braden sat down with Drew in the police station. He shrugged the memory out of his mind. He needed to focus on the present.

"Where have you been?" Drew asked Braden, giving him a speculative look. "There's sand in your hair."

He ran his fingers along his scalp. "I was at the beach."

"Rolling around in the sand? I hope you weren't alone."

He ignored Drew's very interested look. "I came to talk to you about the case."

"Yeah, about that."

Drew glanced toward the Chief Hayes' office. The door was closed, but Braden could see Edwin at his desk. "I was just about to go down the street and grab a coffee. Why don't you come with me?"

Sensing that Drew didn't just want coffee, Braden shrugged. "All right."

Drew grabbed his keys off his desk and they headed out of the station.

"Great day," Drew said as they walked down the street. "I've been inside too much lately. Do you remember when I used to fly down the courthouse steps on my skateboard?" he added, tipping his head to the big building across the street with the long, wide steps.

"I remember that you almost broke your neck

when you decided to skate down the railing," he said dryly.

"Yeah, that was not my wisest move," Drew said with a grin. "Sometimes I can't believe I'm the one who has to arrest the kids making stupid moves now, or that I wear a suit and tie when I walk up those steps."

"Okay, what's going on?" Braden asked as they turned the corner. "You obviously want to tell me something."

"Let's get some coffee first," Drew said. "In the meantime, you can tell me who you were rolling around in the sand with. Or should I just guess?"

Braden didn't bother to answer. He'd stopped telling Drew about girls a dozen years ago, and he saw no reason to start up again.

"What's going on with you and Alexa?" Drew asked, obviously not willing to let the subject drop.

"Who said I was with Alexa?"

"Come on. I'm a detective, and you're not that hard to read. What's up with you two?"

"I don't know," he said honestly. "We've been having some fun together, catching up. Some days it seems like old times. Some days it seems like it's all new."

"You like her," Drew with a confident nod.

"I always liked her," he admitted. "That was never the problem."

"I thought geography was the problem. It's not now."

"It will be. Alexa will go home."

"And you could go anywhere. There's nothing holding you here. Your family would miss you, but I think they'd like to see you happy."

"I'm considering my options," he said, following Drew into a small bakery cafe.

"Are you hungry?" Drew asked. "I'm going to grab a sandwich, too."

"Coffee is fine for me," he said, grabbing a table while Drew placed his order. It was after lunchtime, so the café was empty with the exception of one older man sipping coffee and reading the newspaper.

"So, why are we here?" Braden asked when Drew sat down with two coffees.

"I feel bad that I have to tell you this."

"Tell me what?" he asked, settling back in his chair.

"The Chief had a change of heart. He doesn't want you looking into anything to do with the robbery or the Wellbournes or anyone else. He said he wasn't thinking clearly after finding his dear friend, Phoebe, unconscious and bleeding, and he never should have agreed to involve you. He feels we could muddy the case against whoever is the culprit by not following procedure. He has a point," Drew added.

"So you're firing me?" Braden asked, both amused and a little annoyed. "You're not actually paying me, you know."

"I didn't think it through when I asked you to help. To be honest, part of my motivation was to get you out of your apartment. I thought you'd just look around a little and that would be that. But you've gotten quite involved."

"I have." Braden paused for a long moment. Something wasn't adding up, or maybe it was... "It's funny that you say this now, because I spoke to the Chief yesterday. He seemed fine with me being involved."

"Like I said, he changed his mind."

"After our conversation," he said slowly.

Drew frowned. "What exactly did you say to

him?"

"I asked him about the investigation into Shayla Cummings' death." He tapped his fingers restlessly on the table, feeling like he was missing something. "The Chief was okay with me looking into the break-in at the antique shop, but the fact that I was tying it to the old case was what bothered him. Now, I'm more curious."

Drew sighed, his eyes troubled. "You need to back off, Braden."

"Hey, you got me into this hunt. You wanted me to do something, so I'm doing something. You can't fire me, Drew."

"I'm actually more concerned about getting fired myself."

He didn't want to get Drew into hot water with his boss, but he also wasn't ready to give up on his own private investigation. "I just need to talk a few more people," he said. "I'll be quiet about it."

Drew sighed. "Who?"

"Daniel Stone and Roberta Wellbourne."

"Oh, great. You think you can be quiet investigating a man running for senator and his campaign manager? Come on, Braden."

"I think one of them knows something about Shayla's death. And they're both here in town, at least for the weekend. It's the perfect opportunity."

"I'll do it," Drew said.

"You don't know what I know."

"You don't know anything. You're just operating off gut instinct."

"Okay, you're right, but I want to see it through. I'll talk to them. If nothing comes from that, I'm out."

"You're really enjoying this," Drew said. "Have you thought about going into police work?"

"I don't know."

"You should think about it. You have good instincts and you've been trained to serve and protect. You'd make a great asset to our department – to any department."

"Thanks for joining the list of people trying to find me a new job," he said.

Drew smiled. "It's nice to see you excited about something, even if it may get me fired."

"I'm hoping that won't happen."

"I'm going to do a little more than hope. I'm going to come with you to talk to Daniel Stone."

* * *

Alexa looked around the showroom in the antique shop. She'd finished going through all the boxes and had managed to find places for most of the items. She'd had to consolidate the items on the display shelves and use some of the furniture on sale for storage, but the showroom was feeling more organized. Unfortunately, in all her searching, she hadn't found one damn thing she could imagine anyone wanting to steal. Nor had she found a journal.

The door to the shop opened behind her, and she stiffened, realizing she'd unlocked it during her many trips to the recycle bin in the alley and had not thought to lock it up again. A woman walked into the shop. She wore a beautiful floral dress with a short sweater over the bodice. Her brown hair draped loosely about her shoulders. And she carried a very expensive designer bag.

"I'm sorry, we're not open," Alexa said. "I'm just doing a bit of cleanup."

"Yes, I heard about the robbery the other night. I'm Roberta Wellbourne. I used to be married to Jack Wellbourne. I believe he sent some items to the shop."

Alexa caught her breath, shocked that one of the people she and Braden had put on a list of suspects was actually standing in front of her. "Yes he did. I'm Alexa Parker. My aunt, Phoebe Gray, owns this shop."

"Yes, I know who Phoebe is. Jack became quite fond of her in recent years," Roberta said with an edge of bitterness. "But then there weren't too many women he wasn't fond of. I'd like to see what he sent over."

The question was direct and firm, and Alexa didn't know how she could say no. The items would be on display anyway when Phoebe re-opened the shop. It was also clear that Roberta wasn't leaving until she saw what she'd come to see.

Alexa pointed to the shelves off to the side. "I put most of the items over there. You're welcome to take a look. However, I can't let you take anything with you unless my aunt gives permission."

Roberta's lips drew into a hard line. Alexa doubted that very few people stood up to this woman.

Roberta moved across the room. Her gaze swept across the contents of the shelves. She picked up a music box and opened it, then quickly set it back down. She also looked inside several coffee table books, flipping through the pages, and then putting them down.

"Are you searching for something in particular?" she asked, wondering if Roberta was looking for Shayla's journal.

"Just curious what I didn't get in the divorce," she said coldly.

"Didn't you get divorced a long time ago?"

"Six years," Roberta said, drawing herself up to her full height. "But Jack was very secretive about some of his assets. I always wondered if he was holding something back."

Had Roberta wondered enough to break into the store? But wasn't this a smarter approach, wait for things to get unpacked and then take a look?

"Is this everything?" Roberta asked.

As Roberta asked the question, Alexa suddenly realized it wasn't everything. Her aunt's words rang through her head... *I took one box into the office, and when I came back out someone was in the showroom.*

Alexa had never really looked in the office. She'd grabbed her aunt's purse off the desk and taken it back to the inn with her, but beyond that she'd spent all of her time in the front of the shop.

Roberta's gaze narrowed as the silence went on too long. Alexa cleared her throat. "As far as I know this is it," she said. She had no intention of telling Roberta there was more until she had a chance to look for herself.

Roberta stared at her for another moment, as if she didn't quite believe her, and then returned her gaze to the nearby shelves.

For a few uncomfortable moments, there was nothing but silence between them. Alexa realized she was wasting the perfect opportunity to get more information. She needed to go on the offensive.

"Did you know Shayla Cummings?" she asked.

Roberta flung her a quick look. "Who?"

"Shayla Cummings. She was an actress who rented your beach house for several summers in a row. The last summer she drowned in the sea, not too far away from the house. I'm surprised you wouldn't remember. It was big news."

Roberta drew her tongue along her pink-tinged lips. "Now that you mention it, of course I remember, but that was a long time ago. Why are you asking me about her now?"

"Because Mr. Stone rented the house for Shayla, and you're working for him, aren't you?"

"Are you trying to smear Daniel's reputation?" Roberta asked sharply. "Are you working for his opponent?"

"No, I'm just curious, and I'm not the only one," she added. "The police are interested, too." It was a bit of a stretch to include the police, but she felt she needed some backup.

"The police? Why?"

"Shayla died under mysterious circumstances."

"Well, I'm not sure the circumstances were so mysterious. But I am sure that Daniel had nothing to do with her death. If he rented the house, then it was because Jack asked him to do that."

"Why would Jack make such a request?"

"Because Jack didn't want me to know his lover was renting our house. But he always underestimated me. I knew exactly what he was doing. He wasn't really that smart."

Alexa was surprised that Roberta could speak so coldly and so pragmatically about her husband having an affair. "You don't sound upset about what happened."

"I've had many years to get over it. And it wasn't like she was the first, or the last."

"I'm sorry," she said.

Roberta's eyes widened in confusion. "Sorry about what?"

"That your husband treated you that way."

"You don't need to be sorry for me. You need to mind your own business. Leave the past where it belongs. One girl already ended up dead."

"Is that a threat?" she asked, a shiver running down her spine.

"Don't be stupid. I'm just stating a fact," Roberta said. "And there's no way you'll ever find out what happened to that woman, because the only person who knew the truth is dead. And that was Jack."

"Jack never discussed Shayla's death with you?"

"Her name was never mentioned in our house."

"But you must have been curious when Shayla died. Didn't you wonder what happened?"

"I didn't allow myself to wonder. There was no point," Roberta said.

"Because you didn't want to know if Jack was involved in some way," Alexa said. She could see why Roberta had turned a blind eye. She didn't want her husband's affair to embarrass her.

"No, I didn't want to know," she admitted.

"What about Daniel?"

"I told you. Daniel had nothing to do with Shayla. Leave it alone, Ms. Parker. There's nothing new to be discovered." And with that, Roberta turned and left the shop.

Alexa let out a breath. Roberta Wellbourne was one ice-cold bitch. There was no doubt in Alexa's mind that Roberta would do whatever she needed to do to protect her boss and maybe even her own reputation. But there had also been a ring of truth in her words. Jack was the most likely suspect. And he was dead. But some of his things were here. She headed into the back office to look for the missing box.

Sure enough, as her aunt had said, there was a smaller box tucked underneath the desk. Her pulse began to race. She ripped open the taped top and looked inside. The first items she saw were two heavy, stone bookends. Frowning, her initial enthusiasm began to fade. Jack Wellbourne had had some interesting pieces and also a lot of crap. She suspected this was going to be more of the crap category. She pulled out the bookends, a collection of cigarette lighters, none of which were gold or reminded her of the one she'd seen in the picture with the birthday cake, and three framed watercolors. Letting out a sigh, she realized she'd come up empty again.

The sudden sound of footsteps sent her jumping to her feet. Had Roberta come back to make good on her threat? She really should have locked the front door.

She looked around for some type of weapon and grabbed one of the heavy bookends. She raised it up as the office door opened, then let out a breath as she saw Braden.

His eyes widened. "Sorry, did I scare you?"

She lowered the bookend. "My nerves are on edge. Roberta Wellbourne was just in here."

"What did she want?"

"She wanted to see what stuff her ex-husband had sent over. When I was talking to her, I realized I had forgotten about this box, the one my aunt put here before she was assaulted." She set the bookend down on the desk. "But there was nothing of interest."

"Did you ask Roberta any questions?"

"Yes, and she didn't like them, but she did tell me that Jack and Shayla were having an affair, and that the reason the house was rented in Daniel's name was because Jack didn't want her to know about it. She also mentioned that he was stupid for not realizing she already knew about it. She came across as smart, cold and ruthless. She told me to back off because one girl had already died."

"That sounds like a threat," he said, with concern on his face.

"I think she was trying to scare me, but I'm not sure she'd actually do anything. She seems too cunning to show her hand like that." Pausing, she added, "I told her the police were also investigating. Did you get anything out of Drew?"

"He actually took me off the investigation," Braden replied.

"Why?" she asked with surprise.

"The Chief is afraid I'm going to muck up his case."

"He doesn't have a case."

"I asked him too many questions about Shayla. He didn't like it."

"So that's it?"

"Not a chance," he said with a smile. "I told Drew he couldn't fire me, but since Drew is now concerned about keeping his own job, I let him go with me to see Daniel Stone."

"You saw Daniel Stone?" she asked with surprise.

"For about five minutes," he said. "And I let Drew do the talking. I might have gotten more out of Stone on my own, but I didn't have a choice."

"Did Daniel say anything of value?"

"He confirmed what Roberta told you, that Jack didn't want his wife to know Shayla was renting his house again, so he put Daniel's name on the agreement. Daniel said that he was in New York at the time of Shayla's death, and that he has the proof to back that up. He also told Drew that Shayla had gotten pregnant with Jack's child, and if he looked hard enough, he could probably find medical records attesting to the fact that she'd had an abortion."

"It sounds like he had a lot of answers for five minutes of conversation," she said.

"He was more than prepared. I suspect his

advance people have made sure that he can't be tied to anything connected with Shayla."

"So they're tying Shayla to Jack, which is what Roberta did, too. But Jack is dead. So we may be at the end."

"You're not quitting, are you?"

She was surprised by the challenge in his voice. "Aren't you? Didn't you just get taken off the investigation?"

"We're running our own investigation," he said with a small smile. "Unless you're bailing on me?"

"I'm not bailing, but I have no idea what to do next. Maybe we already have the answer. Jack either killed Shayla, or she killed herself because she was depressed."

"Which means we still have something to figure out."

"It that's even possible."

"If we don't keep looking, we definitely won't find an answer."

She stared back at him, his words resonating with her on a more personal level. "I agree," she said. "The same holds true for us, Braden. If we want to figure out our relationship, we're going to have to keep trying. If we quit now, we're never going to know if we could get it right."

He tensed, his green eyes darkening. "I didn't say I was quitting on us."

"Sometimes, you act like you are."

"Sometimes, you do, too," he said.

"You're right. We both take one step forward and two steps back. We're afraid, because deep down we both know that the connection we have is special." She let out a breath, feeling very emotional all of a sudden. "But I didn't mean to get into all this now. One problem at a time." She put the items she'd just unpacked back into the box. "I think I'll leave this here until I can clear more space in the showroom." As she started to push the box under the desk, her gaze lit on another wooden crate. "What's this?" she muttered.

Braden squatted down. "You found something else?"

"I don't know if it's more Wellbourne stuff or something my aunt is storing."

"Let's find out." He reached under the desk and with a little effort pulled the crate forward.

As she opened the crate, she expected to see more small antique items, but instead she found the remnants of her childhood.

"Oh, my God," she said. Inside was her old backpack, the one she'd worn every day in the summer so she could carry home her treasures after a day of bike riding. There was also her bike helmet, a sketchpad of childish drawings, and an old music box. "Aunt Phoebe kept my things."

Unzipping the backpack, she pulled out a bag filled with her collection of sea glass. Her eyes blurred with tears. "It's all here. She didn't throw anything away."

"She was waiting for you to come back," Braden said.

"I missed so much," she said, feeling incredibly emotional at the reminders of her childhood. "I think back to what my life would have been like if my parents never got divorced, all the happy summers I would have had here." She raised her eyes to his. "I really hate divorce."

"I know," he said quietly. "But you're back now, and maybe you can do something with the sea glass."

"Maybe I can." She stared at the glass for a moment, and then set it aside. There was something else in the backpack – something blue.

Her heart stopped again. "Braden, look." She put her hand around the neck of the shimmering blue bottle and pulled it out, holding it up between them. "The genie's bottle. I forgot all about it. We found it that last day on the beach. We closed our eyes and made a wish..."

She thought about that day, seeing it so clearly and vividly in her mind now. And the wish rang clearly through her head. *I wish Braden would fall in love with me.*

Her breath caught in her throat. Fifteen years later, and she had the same exact wish.

She looked up from the bottle to meet Braden's gaze. There was an odd light in his eyes, as if he were remembering something, too.

"What did you wish for?" she asked.

He shook his head. "I don't remember."

"I think you do."

He drew in a long, slow breath and then let it out. "I wished you would come back, Alexa."

Her heart began to race. "I'm back now, Braden. Your wish came true."

"I guess it did." He stared at her for a long moment and then leaned forward to kiss her.

She put a hand on his shoulder, stopping him. "If you kiss me again, you can't just stop, you can't run off," she warned. "I can't take the back and forth, Braden. You have to decide if you want me or not."

"What do you want, Alexa?" he asked, meeting her gaze

She let a minute tick off the clock, before she said the only thing she could say, "I want you."

He swallowed hard and stood up. "Let's go."

"Where?" she asked, barely getting out the word, as she scrambled to her feet, the bottle still clutched in her hand. She was suddenly afraid to let go of it. Maybe it was the magic of the bottle wrapping around them, pushing them in the direction they were always meant to go.

"To your hotel," he said.

"Really? Are you going to change your mind when the cold air and reality hits you in the face?"

"Are you?" he countered.

"I guess we'll find out."

Chapter Fifteen

Luckily it was a short trip from the antique store to the Cheshire Inn. They didn't speak a word on the way over. Nor did they talk when they took the elevator to the third floor. No words were spoken when she unlocked the door, and they stepped into her room.

Alexa tossed her key down on the dresser, very aware of the king-size bed taking up the center of the room.

Braden had stopped a few feet away from her. She didn't know if he was changing his mind or giving her enough space to change hers.

Tension pulsed in the air between them. She kicked off her flats, then took off her sweater and tossed it over the chair. She felt nervous and excited and worried all at the same time.

Was it too soon? Should they spend more time getting to know each other as adults?

Was it too late? Had they already missed their moment in time?

Were the same doubts going through Braden's mind? She needed him to say something, do something.

Her gaze followed his hands as they moved to the edge of his T-shirt. In one swift action, he pulled the shirt up and over his head, tossing it on the bed.

Her breath caught in her throat as she stared at his beautifully chiseled chest, the fine dark hairs, and the rippled, well-defined muscles. The man had abs.

He also had a long white scar under one rib, a reminder of what he'd been through.

Now she was the one who needed to say something, do something.

He was waiting. He was watching.

God! She was suddenly terrified. She found everything about him incredibly appealing, and she was suddenly very aware of the fact that she hadn't worked out in a few weeks. Would he be disappointed? Would she live up to the fantasy in his mind? Doubt assailed her.

"Don't think so much," Braden said.

Her gaze met his. She licked her lips. "You look really good."

"It's your turn, Alexa," he said.

She wished he would take the decision out of her hands, pull her forward, rip off her clothes, but he seemed far more interested in watching her undress herself.

She'd stripped in front of a man before, but not this man, and all the others seemed hugely unimportant now, as if they'd only been placeholders until she could find Braden again.

She'd found him. She was here. They were both in the same place at the same time.

"I feel like I'm standing on the edge of a cliff," she murmured.

"I'm not going to let you fall," he said.

"No, but you might make me jump."

"Only if you want to."

"I always want to jump when I'm with you – whatever it is we're doing."

"I feel the same way, but if it's too soon –"

She shook her head, cutting him off. "No, it's definitely not too soon." She grasped the edges of her knit top and then pulled it over her head, shaking out her hair as she put her shirt on top of her sweater. She was grateful she'd worn one of her prettier bras for this occasion. The soft pink shell was one of her favorites.

Braden's eyes sparkled. "You're beautiful, Alexa. I knew you would be."

"Did you? I was skinny before." She crossed her arms in front of her waist.

"I like your curves," he said on a husky note. He bridged the gap between them and put his hands on her waist. His fingers were hot against her skin. She could suddenly picture those hands all over her body. "Let's see the rest," he said, pulling the zipper down on her jeans.

She helped him slide her jeans off. Once, free, she kicked them away, meeting Braden for a deep, sensual kiss. There was no hurry now, just desire, intention. Braden was going to make love to her, and he was going to take his time. His lips slid along her jawline, down the curve of her neck. His tongue grazed her collarbone. "You still have some of your freckles," he said, his mouth touching the flurry of light spots along the top curve of her breast.

Her chest was so tight she found it hard to breathe. His slow, sexy, deliberate moves were killing her.

She gripped his shoulders as his tongue slid along the edge of her bra. Her nipples ached, and she almost groaned with relief when he flicked aside the material and his mouth enveloped her nipple.

"Too slow," she muttered.

"Not slow enough," he said, raising his head. He gave her a wicked smile and then dropped to his knees.

Her heart skipped another beat.

He pressed his lips to her belly button, his

fingers flirting with the edge of her lacy thong. And then his mouth followed the same path.

"What's this?" he asked in surprise.

"What?" she asked dazedly. She glanced down and saw his finger tracing the tattoo on her left hip.

"A butterfly, like the ones you used to chase."

"And could never catch," she said. "You used to say I shouldn't try. Some things should be free."

"And you wanted to be free," he said, standing up so he could look into her eyes. "You wanted to be the butterfly. You wanted to fly away from all your problems at home."

"More than anything," she replied. "That urge got stronger after we left here and I became my mother's anchor."

"When did you get the tattoo?"

"After college, after I found out you were married. I went for a long walk on our favorite beach. I knew I couldn't capture the past again, but I wanted that feeling I'd had with you when I was a young girl. I wanted to feel free."

He smiled. "So you put a butterfly on your ass."

"To remind me to fly." She paused. "But I haven't done much flying. I've been too afraid to even look up at the sky. I've just kept my head down and pressed forward like I'm on some long march to nowhere."

"Not anymore," he said firmly. "I want you to fly, Alexa."

"Let's fly together." She pressed her mouth against his and then reached for the snap on his jeans.

They made fast work of the rest of their clothes. Slow and deliberate turned to fast and impatient.

When they were both naked, she smiled in delight. "Wow, I had no idea you were going to grow up to be so hot."

He grinned. "Likewise."

And then they tumbled onto the bed together. They explored each other's bodies with wonder and passion, a mix of the old and the new, the sweet and the sexy. There was none of the usual awkwardness of a first hook up. It was as if they'd been waiting for this moment for fifteen years and their bodies knew exactly what to do. They'd always been in sync. They'd always known what the other was thinking without having to ask. Being with Braden was absolutely and completely right. Alexa felt as if she'd finally come all the way home.

* * *

Alexa woke up hours later. It was night. The hotel room was dark, and the digital clock read eight-fifteen. She didn't want to move. She was very warm and comfortable tucked up against Braden's side, her head on his chest. She could hear the change in his breath, and she lifted her head to look at him.

He opened his eyes and gave her a slow, appreciative smile. "Hey there," he said, his hand running up her bare back. "What time is it?"

"It's after eight o'clock."

His gaze sharpened. "Seriously? We were out that long?"

"Yes, apparently, we were both worn out," she replied, thinking about all the wild and wonderful things they'd done together.

"We had a lot of time to make up for," he said. A hint of doubt entered his eyes. "Was it what you imagined it would be like?"

"It was better, Braden, because it was real. It wasn't a dream where I woke up alone, feeling empty and sad and missing you."

"I had a few of those dreams myself."

Her stomach rumbled, and she flushed with embarrassment. "That wasn't pretty."

He laughed. "I'm hungry, too."

"I wish the inn had room service."

"We can order something in."

She liked the idea that he didn't want to go out, that he didn't want to get dressed and leave her. Now that she had him in her bed, she wasn't eager to let him go. "Delivery sounds good."

"I can recommend the *Hot Wok* if you're interested in Chinese take-out. I'm actually on a first name basis with Han, the owner's son. I've been doing nothing but take-out the last two months. I'll call, if you hand me my cell phone."

She pulled the loose sheet off the bed and wrapped it around her as she searched for his phone.

"Hey, you're blocking my view," he teased from the bed, not looking at all inhibited in his naked pose.

But then why should he try to cover up? He had an amazing body.

"You've seen enough of me for now," she said, tossing him his phone.

"I should be able to say when I've seen enough."

"Just make the call." She used the bathroom, then put on one of the courtesy robes provided by the inn. When she returned to the room, Braden had his boxers on, and was talking on the phone. She sat back down on the bed.

"I hope you ordered plenty of food," she said, as he ended the call. "I'm starving."

"You always could eat a lot for a skinny girl."

"Not so skinny now."

"Stop it, you're gorgeous. I mean it, Alexa. You're pretty from the inside out. You're my summer girl."

She smiled. "I still think you should finish my song."

"Maybe you'll help me write a few more verses."

"Maybe I will," she said.

He leaned over and kissed her. "You know, Han usually takes at least a half hour to deliver."

"Really?" she murmured against his mouth. "How will we pass the time?"

"I've got a few ideas," he said, pulling her on to his lap.

* * *

"Sex, chow mein, late night TV, more sex. What a great night," Alexa murmured as the sun streamed through the window Saturday morning. "What could be better?"

"More sex," Braden suggested with a sleepy smile.

She loved his morning hair, mussed and curling around his face, the dark shadow of beard along his jawline. Most of all she loved waking up next to him. "You have a one track mind," she teased, propping her head up on one elbow as she rolled on to her side to face him.

"Yeah, and you're on it. We're making up for lost time."

"If we're making up for fifteen years, I don't think you'll be leaving for a while."

"Fine with me."

"Seriously, Braden..."

"Seriously?" he teased, turning on his side to look at her. "Should I be worried where this conversation is now going?"

"I just wanted to say that I'm glad you stayed." She thought about how many times she'd wondered during the night if he would be there when she woke up. "I had this terrible feeling, I'd wake up and you'd be gone."

"If I'd wanted to leave, I wouldn't have taken off without a word," he said quietly. "I would have told you. I would have said good-bye. You can trust me, Alexa."

Relief flooded through her. "I want to trust you."

"What's stopping you?"

"All my baggage. My dad didn't sneak out in the middle of the night, but he left really fast, and it took me a long time to come to grips with his absence."

"I understand. You're scared to end up like your mom, but that won't ever happen, Alexa, because you're not her. You're strong, independent, determined. You won't ever let a man break you."

"I hope not. Love scares me. Need terrifies me. I like to have control, because I don't get hurt when I'm in charge."

"You also don't get loved as well. I'm going to try not to hurt you, Alexa."

"I don't know if you realize how much power you have over me, Braden."

"It goes both ways, honey."

She sighed. "I wish we could stay here for a really long time. I don't want to think about the future or the past, I just want to be in this moment and freeze it in time."

"It's Saturday, and even if it wasn't, neither of us is working at the moment. We don't have to go anywhere, do anything, answer to anyone. We're as free as that butterfly on your sexy ass." He gave her a playful swat.

She smiled. "I like you like this, Braden. You're you again. When I first saw you, you were so cold and distant. You were like a stranger to me."

"I'd been living in a fog for months," he admitted. "But being with you again reminded me that life doesn't really suck as much as I thought it did."

She picked up the pillow and playfully hit him with it. "Life doesn't suck? How about a better adjective?"

He put up an arm to ward off her blows. "Okay, being with you is the most amazing, fantastic experience of my life."

"Better," she said, sitting back on her heels.

"Seriously, Alexa."

She licked her lips as his expression grew somber. "Seriously?"

"This *is* the best moment of my life," he said.

"You're exaggerating. It's the after sex glow."

"Then I'll tell you again tomorrow."

"Does that mean we won't be having sex today?" she asked with a grin.

"Not a chance. How do you feel about a shower?"

"I've always wanted someone to wash my hair."

"I'll wash anything you want," he said, grabbing her hand.

They scrambled off the bed and into the bathroom. The shower warmed up fast, steaming up even more as Braden made good on his promise.

* * *

It was afternoon by the time they finally got dressed. Alexa felt the mood slowly change as they put on their clothes. Reality was seeping back in, and she wasn't sure either one of them was ready for it.

Her cell phone rang, making her even more aware of the fact that they were not living on their own desert island. There were other people in the world, people she'd been neglecting, she realized, as she saw the hospital name flash across the screen. She hoped something hadn't gone wrong for her aunt while she was having the time of her life.

"Hello," she said quickly.

"It's Phoebe," her aunt said.

She relaxed at the cheery note in her aunt's voice. "Is everything all right?"

"Just fine, dear. I was wondering if you could do me a favor."

"Anything. What do you need?"

"Could you go by my house and pick up my mail and bring it to me?"

"Of course," she said.

"That would be wonderful. I've been expecting a letter, and the doctor says I can't go home until Monday. I don't know why. I'm doing much better. I feel like my head is starting to clear."

"That's good. I'm so glad. I'll be over in about a half an hour, okay?"

"You don't have to rush. Edwin is on his way. We'll play cards and pass the time. Whenever you get to it is fine."

Alexa hung up the phone and met Braden's questioning gaze. "My aunt wants me to pick up her mail."

"I'll go with you," he said.

"Really? We're doing errands together now?"

He grinned. "See how you have your hooks in me?"

She laughed and followed him to the door.

As she grabbed her key off the dresser, her gaze caught on the shimmering blue bottle. Maybe the magic was finally starting to work.

Chapter Sixteen

Phoebe's home brought to life more memories in Alexa's mind. She'd been in the house six years ago, but she'd spent so much time talking to her aunt that she hadn't really looked around. Now, she decided to take a few moments. She didn't have to go far to hit the past. Her aunt had a wall of photographs in the living room, family members at every stage of their lives.

"I wonder if I'm in any of these," she murmured.

Braden joined her at the wall. "Here you are," he said, pointing to a picture of her with her parents. It was a candid shot taken in the very same living room in which they were standing. There was a Christmas tree in the background, and she was obviously opening one of her presents. Her mother and father were sitting next to each other, and her dad had his arm around her mother's shoulder. They were watching her and smiling. A sudden, sharp pain ran through her.

Braden slipped his arm around her waist. "You, okay?"

"They look happy."

"They do," he said in a neutral voice.

"How can love turn to hate?"

"I don't know, Alexa. Maybe they just didn't fight to stay in love."

"We didn't fight to stay together, either," she said.

He frowned. "Don't compare us to them. That's

your fear talking."

"Don't you have fear? You're just getting out of a marriage. You said you jumped too fast with Kinley. Don't you worry that you could be doing the same thing with me?"

"Our relationship has not been based on speed, Alexa. We've known each other since we were kids."

"No, we knew each other when we were children and we know each other now, but the time in between we were strangers," she corrected.

"It's still different," he said. "Stop looking for problems."

"I can't help it. I feel like us being together again is too good to be true. Is it real? Will it last?"

"Neither life nor love comes with guarantees."

"You're right." She pulled herself together. She would think about their relationship later. Right now, she needed to focus on the present. "I'll get my aunt's mail, and we can go."

The mail drop was in the kitchen, and when she walked into the room she saw a pile of letters on the floor. The mail had obviously been accumulating since her aunt had been taken to the hospital. She picked up the mail and set it on the table. She could at least get rid of the junk before taking everything else to the hospital.

A moment later Braden came into the room with a framed photo in his hand and a frown on his face.

"What's up?" she asked, tossing another credit card offer into the growing junk pile.

"We've been looking at the wrong people," he said cryptically.

"What are you talking about?"

"We've been so focused on who knew Shayla, we forgot to think about who knew Jack." He set the photos down on the table.

In the picture were three people, her aunt Phoebe, Edwin Hayes, and Jack Wellbourne. The photo appeared to have been taken several years ago judging by the clothes.

"Quite a trio," Braden murmured.

She looked up at him in confusion. "I don't get what you're thinking. We already knew that they were friends."

"Jack and Phoebe, yes. Edwin and Phoebe, yes. But not Edwin and Jack. I didn't think about them, and I should have, because the most obvious reason for why the Chief didn't do a more thorough investigation into Shayla's death is Jack."

"You think he covered something up for Jack?"

"The Chief asked Drew to take me off the case right after I talked to him about the investigation into Shayla's death. That seems like a big coincidence to me." Braden pulled out his phone and brought up the Internet. "I need to find out just how well Jack and Edwin knew each other."

While he searched for more information on his phone, she continued sorting the mail. One letter jumped out at her. She had to read the name on the manila envelope twice before she realized she was indeed holding a letter from Jack to her aunt.

"I wonder if this is the letter she was looking for," she muttered.

"Damn, listen to this," Braden interrupted, caught up in his own search. "Jack Wellbourne and Edwin Hayes grew up together in Seattle. They played on the basketball team in high school. They were lifelong friends. And..." he punched the screen. "They were involved in a car accident in college. Edwin credits Jack for saving his life." He raised his gaze to Alexa. "If Jack saved Edwin's life, then wouldn't it make sense that one day Jack would ask his old buddy to return the favor?"

"I don't know," she said, having trouble keeping up with him, because the envelope in her hand was practically burning her fingers. "But this looks like a letter from Jack to my aunt."

Braden set down his phone. "Open it."

"Really?" she asked doubtfully. "It's not addressed to me."

"I don't think your aunt will mind."

She wasn't completely sure about that, but she couldn't resist seeing what Jack had sent to her aunt. So she hoped Phoebe would forgive her.

Slipping her finger under the seal, she pulled out a piece of paper that on first glance appeared to be a list of names and numbers, and bank deposits of some sort. She handed that to Braden while she opened a smaller envelope with a card inside.

"Dear Phoebe," she read aloud. "I asked my lawyer to send you this letter along with the enclosed information after I passed on. The antiques I promised you are coming in a separate shipment. I debated whether or not to share the truth with you, but you've been a good friend to me, and now I must return the favor. Edwin Hayes is not the man you think he is. He wants to marry you and I know that you're tempted to say yes, but you're too good for him, just as you've always been too good for me. Edwin and I have been partners in too many crimes to count. We furthered each other's ambitions. He wanted power. I wanted money. We got both, but I was smarter than Edwin, I kept track of all our deals. He didn't even realize that until just a short while ago. It was almost funny, really. His face was a picture of surprise when I told him. The details are enclosed. I wasn't sure whether or not I should tell you, but I do love you, and I don't want you to end up with a man who is not good enough for you. Do with the information what you want. But now I can rest in peace." Alexa set down the letter. "Wow."

Braden met her gaze. "Edwin and Jack were partners in crime," he said.

"He doesn't mention Shayla's death."

"He didn't have to."

"I did not see this coming," she said. "I guess we were on the wrong track with Roberta Wellbourne and Daniel Stone."

"Yes." Braden glanced down at the paper she'd handed him. "This appears to be a list of bank deposits."

"Payoffs?" She sat up straight as the truth hit her in the face. "Do you realize what this means? Edwin knew Jack had evidence against him."

"And the Chief was the one who found your aunt," Braden said, following her train of thought.

"Maybe he didn't find her. Maybe he's the one who put her in the hospital." She jumped to her feet. "He's with her now. We have to go."

"He won't hurt her, Alexa. He loves her."

"Based on what Jack said in his letter, I'm not sure he loves anyone but himself."

* * *

Alexa held her breath on the quick trip across town to the hospital. She read Jack's letter again and took a longer look at the evidence he'd presented. It appeared from the notes and the expenses that Jack had been paying Edwin off for years. As she ran down the ledger, her gaze settled on one entry that simply said *Shayla*.

"It's here," she said to Braden. "I found Shayla's name and next to it is $20K. He paid Edwin off for something."

"Silence or a short investigation," Braden offered.

She flung him a quick glance. "I hope it wasn't for killing her." Her stomach felt sick at the thought of her aunt alone with a possible murderer.

"We don't know that it went that far."

"We don't know that it didn't."

After parking the car, they raced into the hospital and rushed up the stairs to Phoebe's room.

Her aunt looked up in surprise. Edwin Hayes was standing next to her, holding a pillow in his hands.

"What are you doing? Put that down," Alexa said, charging across the room. She grabbed the pillow out of his hands, ignoring his shocked look.

"Alexa, what on earth is going on?" Phoebe asked. "Edwin was just adjusting my pillows."

"Are you sure?" she asked.

"I don't understand," Phoebe said in confusion.

"Ask him," she said, tipping her head to Edwin. "Ask him what he knows about Jack and Shayla and the break-in at your shop."

Edwin's face paled, and Alexa could see the truth and guilt in his eyes.

"You know," he said.

"Know what?" Phoebe interrupted. "Someone tell me what is going on."

Alexa put the pillow on the foot of the bed and handed her aunt the envelope. "Jack Wellbourne wrote you a long letter. Is this what you were waiting for?"

Phoebe gave her a confused look. "No, I was waiting for a letter from my friend, Doris. She's supposed to pick me up some art while she's in France." Phoebe turned the letter over in her hands.

"You opened this?"

"I'm sorry, but I saw Jack's name and I just couldn't stop myself." Alexa saw Edwin glance from her to the door, but Braden was standing in the way. There was no way out, and the realization was in the older man's eyes. "This letter is what you were looking for in the antique shop, wasn't it?" she asked him.

Edwin didn't answer, but when Phoebe moved to open the envelope, he held up a hand. "Wait," he said. "Let me tell you in my own words."

"Tell me what?" Phoebe asked.

"You know Jack and I grew up together."

"Yes, of course. He saved your life when you were in college," Phoebe said.

"He did, but that wasn't the whole story."

"Why are you telling me this now?" Phoebe asked, a frown on her face.

"Because if I don't, Jack will tell you – or they will," he replied. "I've made some mistakes, Phoebe."

"Big ones," Alexa put in.

"Yes, big ones," Edwin echoed. "And they all started with Jack and that crash. Will you let me tell you, Phoebe?"

"Of course," she said quietly, setting down the letter.

"Jack was driving drunk, and I was in the passenger seat. I didn't realize how wasted he was until we were on the road. We hadn't been together the whole night, so I had no idea he wasn't okay to drive. He crashed the car, and then he pulled me out of it just before the car caught fire. I would have been dead if it hadn't been for him. He asked me to lie, to say that I was driving. He couldn't afford to get a DUI. He said I owed him, and I couldn't deny that. So I lied. That was the beginning. Then there were more favors, things Jack needed me to do for him. In return, he paid me cash. I didn't make much, and my wife had expensive taste. So it didn't seem like that bad of a bargain."

"What kinds of things were you doing for him?" Phoebe asked.

"Just small stuff in the beginning, fixing a speeding ticket, that kind of thing." Edwin took a breath and then continued. "Then Jack got me the job here in Sand Harbor. He was buying up a lot of real estate, and he pretty much wanted to run this town. He thought it would be good to have me in the department. I liked Sand Harbor. I thought my wife would be happy here, too. But then there were more favors."

He drew in a deep breath. "Jack called me in the middle of the night one August and told me that a woman staying in his house had overdosed. I went over there and found Shayla dead on the bed. Jack swore he hadn't killed her. He showed me her suicide note. I believed him. I knew that Shayla was distraught. I'd spoken to her a few days earlier, trying to get her to move on with her life. I was afraid for her. I could see that Jack's refusal to leave his wife was hitting her hard. But she was furious. She screamed at me."

"You were the person Shayla was fighting with," Alexa interrupted. "Braden and I heard the fight. She threw something at you."

"I didn't know anyone heard our argument," Edwin said.

"We were on the beach," she said.

"Go on," Braden ordered.

Alexa glanced at her aunt, hoping the news wasn't stressing her out too much. "Are you all right?" she asked.

Phoebe nodded, her face pale, but her gaze determined. "I need to hear the rest."

"Jack didn't want Shayla's body found in his house," Edwin said. "He was desperate to get her out of there. If he hadn't been so panicked, if I'd thought for more than five minutes, I would not have agreed to his plan."

"Which was what?" Alexa asked.

"Jack and I took her body out in his boat and dumped her overboard about two miles off shore. We thought it was far enough, but three days later, her body washed up on the beach. It was like she was coming back to taunt us. I had to scramble to tone down the investigation. There was a lot of press here asking questions. But I had to protect Jack, because I had to protect myself. Jack had a lot more on me than just Shayla's death."

"Why didn't the drugs show up in the autopsy?" Braden interjected.

"I made sure they didn't," Edwin said flatly.

"You had a lot of power," Braden put in.

"And I used it," Edwin replied. He turned back to Phoebe. "I knew that Jack didn't want me to have you. He saw us getting close, and he didn't like it. He had so much more than me, but it was never enough. Last year he asked me to back away. I refused him. It was the first time in a very long time that I'd said no. Part of my bravery came from the fact that he was dying. I didn't think he'd be able to hurt me any more, but right before he passed, he told me he was going to make sure that I never got you, because you were too good for me. When I heard he'd sent you boxes of stuff from the house, I thought he'd sent you the evidence he'd been holding all these years – his insurance, as he liked to call it."

"So you broke into the shop?" Phoebe asked,

anger edging her tone.

"Yes, I broke the glass in the door, because I wanted it to look like vandalism. I didn't know you were there, Phoebe. I saw you earlier that night. You didn't say you were going down to the store."

"It was an impulsive decision," Phoebe said.

"You came out of the back room, and I didn't know it was you at first. It was dark. Why didn't you turn on the lights?"

"I was about to, when I saw something bright."

"It was probably my flashlight. I moved forward, and you screamed. You jumped backward, and you hit your head on the counter. There was so much blood. I was afraid you were dead. I called for help, and I held you in my arms until the paramedics came."

"And then you stayed by my side to make sure I didn't remember," Phoebe said harshly.

"No, I stayed by your side to make sure you were all right. I am so, so sorry about what I did. You are the last person I wanted to hurt. I love you, Phoebe."

"I don't even know who you are," she said in bewilderment. "You're a police officer. You're supposed to protect people, not commit crimes."

"You'll know who I am when you read Jack's letter," he told her sadly. "I started down a path I couldn't get off of a very long time ago. I was hoping I could turn things around, begin again with you, especially after Jack died. No one else ever had to know. But he couldn't let me slide. I'm sorry, Phoebe."

"You should have told me, Edwin. You should have just come clean and said something instead of breaking into my shop."

"That was a dumb move. I should have realized that Jack would make sure you got the letter directly and not just by chance."

"If you'd asked me if you could look in the boxes, I would have let you."

"I was afraid you'd find the evidence first. It was self preservation."

Alexa turned around as the door opened. She was surprised to see Drew walk into the room.

"I texted him," Braden explained, answering her unspoken question. "And I've been recording this conversation while you were on speaker," he added, holding up his phone.

"Looks like we have some talking to do, Chief," Drew said heavily.

"Yes," Edwin said, with defeat in his voice. He gave Phoebe one last look. "Is there any chance you won't read that letter?"

"I'm sorry, Edwin," she said with teary regret.

"Okay," he said with a tight nod. "Then I'll say goodbye."

Phoebe didn't answer, and after a moment, Edwin walked out of the room, followed closely by Drew.

Alexa sat down on the bed. "You don't have to read the letter now. It doesn't say anything that Edwin didn't already tell you. In fact, it says less."

"I wonder what's going to happen to him," Phoebe said.

"He's going to pay for his crimes," Braden said, stepping up to the bed. "It's just too bad that Jack didn't have to pay for his."

"I always knew there was something between those two, something deep and dark," Phoebe said. "That's why I never said yes to either one of them. I was leaning a little in Edwin's direction, but something held me back, and now I know it was his secret. He couldn't let me all the way in, and you can't have love without truth."

"I'm sorry, Aunt Phoebe," Alexa said.

"I'll survive. I'm a tough, old broad," she said with a sigh. She handed Alexa back the letter. "I think you should give this to Drew. I don't need to be involved. I'm moving on. At least, I will be moving on when I can get out of this bed."

"Soon," Alexa promised. She handed Braden the envelope. "Can you take care of this? I want to stay with my aunt for a while."

He nodded. "I'll see you both later."

Phoebe smiled at her after Braden left the room. "He's still sweet on you," she said.

"I'm pretty sweet on him, too," she replied.

"So what happens now?" Phoebe asked.

"That's what I need to figure out."

"Can I make a suggestion?"

"Sure."

"Don't let him go, Alexa. Braden is a good man. But most importantly, he's *your* man. He always has been."

* * *

Alexa waited for Phoebe to fall asleep and then headed back to the inn. She picked up the genie's bottle and took it down to the beach where she'd first found it. The sun was sinking low in the horizon, the way it had been that last summer day of her youth. She sat down and dug her toes into the sand, gazing out at the horizon.

Phoebe had told her to hang on to Braden, and that's exactly what she wanted to do, but she had to make sure that he wanted to hang on to her. She glanced down at the bottle and smiled. "If you still have any power," she said, "I could still really use that wish."

A man flopped down beside her. *Braden.* She wasn't really surprised.

"You found me," she said.

"I went by the hospital, the inn, and the antique shop. I figured you'd end up here."

"Sorry. I was going to text you, but I just needed a few minutes."

"Do you want me to go?" he asked.

She shook her head. "No." She took a breath for courage and then said, "I don't ever want you to go, Braden. I love you."

Emotion darkened his eyes. "I love you, too, Alexa."

"What do we do now?"

"What we don't do is say goodbye. You were right earlier when you said we were going to have to stick it out and fight for what we wanted. I'm ready to do that. It doesn't have to be here in Sand Harbor. It can be in San Francisco. Wherever you're going, I'm going with you. The beauty of not having a job or a career plan is that I can be with you wherever you want to be, Alexa."

"But I want you to have a life you want, too."

"We'll figure it out together. I know you have plenty of ideas," he said with a teasing smile.

"Mostly bad ones," she said.

"I liked some of your bad ones last night."

She flushed. "We are not talking about that."

"I like that you still have innocence about you," he said quietly.

"Innocence? I haven't felt innocent in a very long time."

"Maybe that's the wrong word. Maybe it's hope I see in your eyes," he said. "You always wanted to believe in the power of love. Even when your parents were verbally beating each other up, you still wanted to believe that somehow things would work out."

"But they didn't."

"Not for them. For us, it will be different."

"I want to believe that."

"Then believe, because I want to marry you, Alexa. I want to make you mine. I want to have children with you, make a home, live a life that's full and rich and that's ours. We've spent too much time in our parents' shadows. This is our time."

His words touched her heart and she found her eyes blurring with happy tears. "I want all of what you just said."

He leaned over and gave her a tender kiss.

Then he tipped his head to the bottle and said, "So why did you bring the bottle out here?"

"I wasn't sure until just this second," she replied. "Until my wish came true. You told me you loved me, Braden, and that was my wish, my twelve-year-old wish. It took you long enough."

"I loved you then, too, Alexa. I just didn't have the courage to say it."

"Now that both of our wishes have come true, I'm going to throw the bottle back in the sea."

"I like that," he said with approval.

"Because we don't need wishes anymore, we have each other," she said, as she got to her feet. "Want to help me?"

They walked down to the shoreline. "You have a better arm," she said, handing Braden the bottle. "I hope the bottle brings someone else their greatest wish."

Braden drew back his arm and made a very long throw. The bottle splashed into the water and the sea took it down.

"I wonder if the bottle will come out the same," she murmured. "Or if the ocean will turn it into new glass."

"You definitely have to learn how to make glass, Alexa."

"I have my first lesson tomorrow," she said.

"What about San Francisco?"

She shrugged. "We'll figure out my job after we come up with a career for you – rock star, auto mechanic, astronaut, pro baseball player, cop..."

He cut her off with a kiss. "Actually, the cop part sounds kind of interesting."

She gave him a knowing look. "I think so, too. I might want to stay here, Braden. I like Sand Harbor."

"I like it, too, but I love you more, so we'll figure it out -- what's best for both of us."

She slipped her hands into his. "You were my first kiss, Braden."

He smiled down at her. "And you were mine."

"That kiss was perfect," she said.

"This one is going to be even better." And he touched his mouth to hers.

THE END

I hope you enjoyed JUST A WISH AWAY! Book Three in the Wish Series will be out in the summer of 2012.

Continue reading for excerpts from Book #1 in the Wish Series, A SECRET WISH.

EXCERPT - A SECRET WISH (#1, Wish Series)

Chapter One

Liz Kelly stepped up to the waist-high ledge that ran around the tenth-floor roof of St. John's Hospital. Although the roof was a popular retreat for doctors and nurses on break, it was quiet on this Friday night. Just past seven o'clock, anyone not on duty had already left the building, trying to get one last warm and sunny weekend in before fall turned into winter. She loved the view from the roof, especially as night settled over the city. From her vantage point, she could see the cable cars chugging up and down the steep hills of San Francisco, the colorful sails on the boats in the Marina, and the lights of the Golden Gate Bridge blazing through a bank of fog hovering over the ocean.

The view always inspired her. Up here she felt like she could be anyone and do anything. Unfortunately, she couldn't seem to turn the inspiration into action. As soon as she went back inside, she returned to her old ways, to her safe, risk-free existence that was getting her nowhere. She liked being a nurse, but the rest of her life was in shambles. She'd lived with a half dozen roommates in the last decade, changed apartments three times, and had just been dumped by her boyfriend of three years.

What annoyed her most was that Kyle had broken up with her. She should have been the one to break up with him. He'd fallen far short of her expectations, but she'd never been able to pull the trigger on their relationship. She'd always been afraid of being thirty and alone. Well, that's exactly what had happened. But tonight was the start of a new decade. She needed to get it together, take a risk, and stop being paralyzed by fear of making the wrong decision. She had to take charge of her life and stop letting her future be defined by her past. She needed to do something...

What that *something* was, she wasn't quite sure, but she intended to find out.

Mental pep talk over, she opened a small bakery box from Faith's Fancies and slid out a miniature gourmet cupcake dotted with pink icing and chocolate stars. Chocolate was her passion, especially rich, dark chocolate. Taking a pink candle out of her purse, she stuck it in the icing, and raised the cake to the starlit sky. "Happy birthday to me."

Her muttered words seemed to mock her newfound resolve, so she raised her voice and shouted, "Did you hear that, San Francisco? Today, Elizabeth Karen Kelly is thirty years old and ready to take on the world."

She smiled, feeling silly but also energized. She pulled out a pack of matches from her bag and lit the candle, holding her hand around the flame so the wind wouldn't blow it out while she was thinking of a wish.

As much as she wanted love, she was also scared of being vulnerable. She'd loved her father and he'd turned out to be a horrible person. She'd loved her mother and had been left behind. She'd picked Kyle because he was solid and stable and seemed like the anchor she needed in her life. But Kyle hadn't just held her down; he'd held her back.

If Prince Charming couldn't find her, perhaps she needed to find him. Drawing in a deep breath, she

made a secret wish. *Someone for me to love.*
A gust of wind came up, blowing out the flame
before she could do so. Probably a sign that her wish
had not been heard. She felt an unexpected surge of
disappointment.

That was the problem with hope... it made the fall
back to reality even worse. She should know better.
She pulled out the candle and licked the icing from it.

"Is that it?" a man asked.

She jumped at the unexpected voice, the cupcake
flying out of her hand and over the side of the building.
She stared in bemusement at the man who'd appeared
out of nowhere. He was tall, with sandy blond hair, and
was dressed in jeans, a white T-shirt with *Stanford*
emblazoned across the front, and a brown leather
jacket.

"You scared me," she said, her heart beating way
too fast.

"Sorry." He gave her a smile. "So was that the
extent of your celebration?"

"Uh." She glanced over the ledge, realizing her
cupcake was long gone. "I guess so, since you made
me drop my cake. What are you doing out here? Didn't
you see the sign that said *Employees Only?*"

"I don't pay much attention to signs."

"So you're a rule breaker."

"When necessary. I needed some air. Sorry about
the cupcake," he added.

"It was going to be really good, too," she said with
a wistful sigh.

"How old are you today?"

"I'm thirty – the big three-O. I don't know why
they call it that. It's not as if O stands for orgasm."
*Good grief. Had she said that out loud? For some
reason, good-looking men made her jump into nervous
conversation.*

He gave her an odd look, probably wondering who would want to give her three orgasms.

She put up a hand. "Don't worry. I wasn't asking for volunteers."

"That wasn't what I was thinking."

"Yeah, right. You looked like a deer caught in the headlights."

His smile widened. "Not true. So why are you out here by yourself on your birthday? You're too pretty not to have friends."

Her cheeks warmed as his gaze swept across her face and figure. She couldn't help wishing that she'd retouched her makeup, taken her brown hair out of its practical ponytail, and changed out of her loose, ill-fitting scrubs. Not that it mattered. She'd probably never see him again.

"Good line," she said. "You're a charmer."

"You don't like compliments."

"I don't like men who psychoanalyze me in the first five minutes of meeting me," she countered.

His grin broadened. "Got it. But you still haven't answered my question. Why the solo celebration?"

She didn't know why she felt the need to explain her pathetic party – maybe so it wouldn't look so pathetic. "My best friend just had a baby. Another one is on her honeymoon, and a third is home sick with the flu. I do have friends. They're just not available right now." Actually, her friends were rarely available these days. They'd moved on with their lives – getting married, having children – while she'd been treading water or trying to make things happen with Kyle. "And birthdays are not that big a deal," she added.

"I like birthdays. They're a good time to make a resolution."

"Isn't that what New Year's Eve is for?"

"Who says you can only make a resolution once a

year?"

"No one, but I don't have much luck with the resolutions I do make. They usually involve losing twenty pounds, and so far I haven't managed to make that happen. I have a terrible chocolate addiction. If only they made a patch for that, I'd be set." *Great! Now she'd just pointed out that she needed to lose twenty pounds. No wonder she had trouble getting a man.*

"A resolution doesn't have to be about a diet," he said. "Last year I ran a marathon. The year before that I parachuted out of an airplane."

"Well, aren't you quite the hero." She wasn't sure if he was spinning her a line, but he certainly looked fit enough to run a marathon and young enough to taunt death by jumping out of an airplane. "What are you going to do this year?"

"Sail under the Golden Gate Bridge."

"That sounds like fun. When's the big day?"

"Tomorrow. But I'm much younger than you – I'm only turning twenty-nine."

"Ah, twenty-nine – I remember it well."

He laughed. "It was only what, twelve hours ago?"

"About that. Do you know how to sail?"

"No. Will that be a problem?"

She couldn't help but smile back at him. His candor was refreshing, and she started to relax. "It might be. But something tells me you're pretty good at getting what you want."

"I used to be," he said, his tone turning somber. "I was the guy who had everything. Charmed."

"And charming."

He tipped his head. "I try."

"So what happened to that guy?"

"Life." A small sigh followed his words. Before she could ask what it meant, he added, "Are you a nurse here?"

"No, I just love to wear these baggy blue shirts and pants."

"Right. Stupid question." He paused. "How do you do it?"

"Do what?"

"Watch people die."

The change in subject surprised her. "Not everyone dies. Most people live."

"My father died here. It was long. Painful. Horrible. I'll never forget it."

She met his gaze head on. "I'm sorry."

"I bet you say that a lot."

"I still mean it." She knew what it was like to lose a parent. And it didn't matter how old you were.

"I was with my father when he passed. He fought for months to recover, but he couldn't beat the cancer. Even though I knew the end was coming, and I was relieved that there would be an end to his pain and suffering, it was still shocking when it happened. One minute he was there, then he was gone…" He cleared his throat. "Hell of a birthday conversation. I apologize again."

"That's all right. Now I understand why you needed some air."

"The hospital smell sticks to my clothes. How do you take it?"

"You get used to it."

"Are you off duty?"

"Yes."

"Why don't I buy you a drink to toast your birthday?"

"Uh…" She didn't know what to say. It wasn't as if she had other plans, but he was a stranger.

"I promise, no more depressing conversation. We'll have a drink in honor of your new decade. I might even buy you another cake."

"I don't know you."

"That makes it better, doesn't it?" he said with a challenging smile. "You can let your hair down. Be whoever you want to be."

She had no idea who that person would be, but the idea was definitely appealing. Still, old habits died hard. "I should say no."

"Why?"

"Because it's not smart to go out with a perfect stranger. You could be an axe murderer or a serial killer or a life insurance salesman."

His deep, infectious laugh lit up the night, and his sparkling eyes made her feel like she'd been kicked in the stomach – or swept off her feet.

"I'm not any of those things."

"And you'd tell me if you were?"

"Good point, but isn't thirty about facing your fears? It's just a drink in a public place. Unless you're scared of a pina colada?"

"Why would you *ever* think I would order a pina colada?"

"Because you're too funny and honest to be the martini type."

"Which is what?"

"Sophisticated, brittle, phony laugh, dyed blonde hair, icy blue eyes, doesn't really give a damn about anyone but herself."

"That certainly rolled right off your tongue," she said, giving him a thoughtful look. "Why do I get the feeling you're describing someone in particular?"

"Guilty." He paused. "Get a drink with me and prove me wrong."

She hesitated. "I don't have anything to prove."

His gaze met hers and for some reason she had the feeling he could read her mind. "Don't you?"

His challenge hung in the air for a long minute. Of course she had something to prove. She was going to change her life. And what better way to start than to do something she wouldn't normally do?

Besides that, she was intrigued by and attracted to this man, this stranger, who'd appeared out of nowhere. The idea crossed her mind that maybe he'd been sent to fulfill her birthday wish, but that was a foolish thought. He'd just lost his dad after a terrible illness. He'd come up to the roof to catch his breath. He hadn't come for her. It was purely coincidence.

"What's your name?" he asked.

She drew in a deep breath, feeling like she was about to cross over a line she couldn't cross back. But if she was ever going to take a chance, it might as well be now.

"Liz," she said. "My name is Liz. And I'd like that drink."

* * *

"Surprise! Happy birthday!"

Angela Payne stopped just inside the front door of her three-bedroom apartment in San Francisco's Sunset District. Smiling faces appeared from behind every piece of furniture, each one looking more sheepish than the next. She inwardly sighed. They should feel guilty. She'd told everyone that she didn't want a party to celebrate thirty-five. Time was not her friend, but her large Italian family turned every holiday or occasion into a party. The dining room table was laden with food, and music played loudly over the speakers. Judging by her Uncle Rico's red face, the wine was already flowing.

"I'm sorry. I tried to stop them," her husband Colin whispered as he kissed her on the cheek. "But your mother is a force of nature."

Looking at her five-foot-three-inch mother, Mary Margaret Razzini, no one would believe she was a force of anything, but her personality was much bigger than her stature. Angela had never yet won a battle where her mother was concerned, and she'd had far more practice than Colin.

Her mother lifted her chin, planted her hands on her waist, and said firmly, "It's your birthday, Angela. Of course you must have a party." She waved her hands in the air as she always did when she spoke. "I made three kinds of lasagna. You'll eat, you'll laugh, and you'll have fun. Mama knows best." Her mother turned her head sharply as one of the grandchildren tugged on her skirt. "Yes, yes, Jimmy. I will get you some lemonade." She headed off to the kitchen, as if she owned the place.

"I'll help her," Colin said quickly, disappearing before she could remind him that the only request she'd made for her birthday was to have a private dinner with him. She had things she wanted to discuss, but not in front of her family.

"Try the shrimp cheese puffs," Lisa said, holding up a silver tray. "I made them myself."

She stared down at her petite, dark-haired sister and gave her a glare. "I told you I didn't want a party."

"It makes Mama happy to take care of you. She's been so lost since Daddy died."

"Daddy died nine years ago. When are you going to stop offering that excuse for everything Mama does that we don't like?"

"She still misses him," Lisa said with a shrug. "Try one of my puffs."

Angela popped a shrimp cheese puff into her mouth. It was hot, tangy, and delicious. "Not bad."

"Not bad?" Lisa echoed in annoyance. "They're

spectacular. And who are you to criticize, anyway? You can't even make good spaghetti sauce. You're lucky Colin can cook, or you'd starve to death." She smiled at her younger sister's predictable reaction. Pushing Lisa's insecurity button was an old habit and probably one she should have outgrown by now. "I was just kidding. The puff is fabulous." It was true that she couldn't cook like her two sisters and her mother. But then, she'd always been the odd one out, a tall, blue-eyed blonde in a sea of dark-eyed brunettes, some latent gene from her grandmother. She preferred painting to cooking. She was the artist in the family, the one who lost track of time while sketching a picture, the one who had no domestic talents. Fortunately, her husband didn't mind cooking or eating take-out.

"I also made the cannelloni," Lisa added, waving her hand toward the dining room table where most of the party was gathered. "It's better than Gina's, but don't tell her I told you that."

"Believe me, I won't." Gina and Lisa had competed with each other for as long as she could remember, and she'd always been caught in the middle, each one wanting her to take their side. "David must count his lucky stars every day that he married you," she said, popping another puff into her mouth. She waved to David, who was sitting on the couch with one of his two children on his lap. His belly hung over his belt, a definite sign that he'd been sampling more than a few of Lisa's puffs.

"David is driving me crazy," her sister confided. "He wants me to have another baby, as if we don't have our hands full with the ones that we–" She bit off the end of her sentence, her brown eyes darkening. "Sorry, Angie."

"It's fine," she said quickly, not wanting to get

into that subject.

"It's not fine, and I shouldn't have said anything."

"What's going on?" Gina asked, interrupting their conversation. She handed Angela a glass of wine. "What's the look on your face about? You can't possibly be that mad about the party."

She really didn't want to talk to Gina tonight. Whereas Lisa was insecure about her choices, her older sister Gina was always right. She had a strong personality and never had any trouble expressing her opinions, which made her a very good lawyer but not the nicest person to be around.

"Would it matter if I was?" she asked.

"Mama is the one who gave birth to you. If she wants to celebrate your birthday, you should smile and say thank you," Gina told her. "She went through eighteen hours of labor to bring you into the world. That was no picnic."

Her gut tightened. No matter what conversation she seemed to be in, it always came down to babies. "I have to wash my hands," she muttered.

As she walked away, she could hear Lisa telling Gina how stupid she was to bring up the subject of their mother giving birth, and Gina replying, "For God's sake, doesn't Angela ever think about anyone but herself?"

This was exactly why she hadn't wanted a party. She loved her family, but lately she couldn't stand being around them. Her sisters and cousins were all married. They had children. Some even had teenagers. She was so far behind the curve it was ridiculous. She was jealous. She knew it. They knew it, too.

In the bathroom, she closed the door and stared at her face in the mirror. She'd never imagined she'd be thirty-five and without a baby. But three attempts at in-vitro fertilization had left her with an empty womb and a bankrupt savings account. Time was running out. She might have only one more chance. Colin had recently received a big bonus at work, and she knew just how she wanted to spend the money. She had hoped to talk to him about it tonight, but that would have to wait until they were alone. She certainly didn't want any input from her mother or her sisters.

She washed her hands, splashed water on her face, and reapplied her lipstick. She was too thin, too pale. She'd always had a tendency to wear her stress on her face and today it was all there. She forced a smile. She just had to get through the next few hours. Her family had gone to a lot of trouble for her. She had to at least pretend to be happy. As Gina said, it wasn't always about her.

Leaving the bathroom, she walked down the hall and into the dining room. Colin was filling a plate at the buffet table. At forty, her husband could still make her heart skip a beat. He was a very attractive man, tall and lean, with light brown hair and golden brown eyes. He'd taken off his suit jacket, loosened his tie, and rolled the sleeves of his white dress shirt up to his elbows. His hair was mussed. He had a habit of running his fingers through it whenever he was tired or worried. She could always tell what kind of day he'd had by the way his hair looked. Tonight it was a mess, probably because her mother had railroaded him into throwing her a surprise birthday party.

Turning, he caught her watching him and gave her an apologetic smile. "I made this for you, Angie."

She walked over and took the plate out of his hands. "Thanks."

He handed her a fork. "No knife for you. I'm afraid you'll use it on me."

"Good thinking."

"Your family loves you so much. They wanted to

make you happy. I got swept up in their enthusiasm. By the time your mother finished talking to me, I was convinced that throwing you a surprise party was the best idea in the world, until you walked through the door a few minutes ago."

"It's okay. Your intentions were good." She looked around the crowded apartment, knowing she was lucky and blessed. "Everyone wants me to be happy, including you, and I have an idea about that."

"So do I. Come with me." Colin led her into the kitchen, which was surprisingly empty. He took an envelope out of the drawer and handed it to her. "This is your real birthday surprise."

Her pulse leapt with expectation. "What's this?"

"Your present. I've been thinking about what to do with that bonus I got from work, and I came up with the perfect idea."

"Me, too," she said, meeting his gaze. "I wanted to talk to you about it tonight. It seems like fate that your bonus is exactly the amount we need to…" She opened the envelope, expecting to see a letter with an appointment time at the fertility clinic, like so many they'd received in the past. Instead, she saw tickets – tickets to some sort of cruise.

"The Caribbean," Colin said with excitement in his voice. "Ten days cruising the high seas, just you and me. Miles of ocean, music, casino action, and all the food you can eat. It will be a second honeymoon, a new start. We can talk about what we want to do with the rest of our lives."

"You spent your bonus on a cruise?" she asked in shock.

"Yes. Why?" His smiled dimmed. "What's wrong, Angie?"

She looked into his eyes, wondering how he could possibly be confused about her reaction. "I thought we would use the money to try IVF one more time. It's the exact amount we need."

The blood drained out of his face. His jaw tightened. "We agreed that we were done after the last time."

"We didn't agree. We just ran out of money. But now we have the money."

He shook his head. "It's not about the money. It's about you and me. I can't watch you go through it again. I can't see the hope in your eyes and then the despair. I'm afraid one of these days you'll break, and I won't be able to put you back together. Some things are not meant to be. We have to accept it."

"The doctor still thinks it could happen for us. I'm only thirty-five. There's still time – but not a lot of time. Each year the odds go down."

"You hear what you want to hear. The doctor told you it might never happen, Angie."

"He also said it might," she argued. "How can you give up?"

He put his hands on her shoulders, gazing into her eyes. "We're happy, aren't we? We love each other. We have good friends, family, nieces and nephews to spoil. You have your gallery, your painting. Why can't that be enough for you?"

"Because it can't." She stepped away from him, unable to bear his touch. He was trying to take away her dreams.

"You have to be realistic–"

"No, I need to have a baby. And I don't want to look back in five years and say, What if I had just tried one more time? Don't you think we owe it to ourselves to take one last chance?"

He stared at her for a long moment. She wanted to see him weaken, watch the reassuring smile come into his eyes and spread across his face. She wanted him to say, "Yes, that's what I want, too."

"I can't."

His words didn't register for a moment, but slowly they sank in. His expression was definite, unyielding. God! *He wasn't going to change his mind.* A feeling of desperation swept over her. *Was this it? Was this really the end?* If Colin wouldn't agree to the insemination, they were done. It was over. She would never have a baby. She would never feel that tiny life inside her. She pressed her hand to her empty womb, an ache spreading down deep in her soul.

She'd touched her sisters' pregnant stomachs many times, feeling the kicks and flutters of their babies, and she'd wanted that incredible and special feeling inside her own body. She'd always thought she'd have that moment. The idea that she wouldn't was too much to handle. She felt like she couldn't breathe, as though the walls were closing in on her.

"It will get easier," Colin told her, a hint of desperation in his voice. "We'll fill up our days. We'll make ourselves happy. It will be all right."

Before she could say anything else, the kitchen door flew open and her mother walked in, holding a cake lit up with candles. Her sisters, their husbands, their children, and the rest of the party crowded into the small kitchen.

She stared down at the cake, the blaze of thirty-five candles surrounding the words *Happy Birthday Angela.*

"Make a wish," her mother said, setting the cake down on the table in front of her.

She had tried wishing. It didn't work. But everyone was waiting. They were calling out suggestions for wishes... *A new car... A trip around the world.* They were suffocating her with their desire to have her move on, give up her dream and wish for something that wouldn't take a miracle. Then they could go on, too. They wouldn't have to watch what they said or worry about her.

She had to give them what they wanted. It was what she always did.

But when she closed her eyes to make her secret wish there was only one thought in her mind.

Please, God, give me a baby.

She blew out the candles to applause and laughter and an off-key version of *Happy Birthday*. Her mother suggested they take the cake back out to the dining room to cut it, and Angela was grateful when the group moved out of the kitchen, leaving her and Colin alone again.

He gave her a pleading look, silently begging her to stop arguing, to accept what was done. "Let's get some cake," he said. "It's your favorite."

"I'm not hungry."

Her Uncle Rico popped back into the room. "We need more wine, Colin. Time for the secret stash every good Italian keeps down in the cellar."

"I don't have a secret stash or a cellar," Colin said. "But the liquor store down the street has plenty of wine."

"I'll go." Angela grabbed the excuse like a lifeline. She had to get out of this room, out of this party, out of this life.

"You can't leave – it's your party. I'll go," Colin said.

"No, I need some air."

He frowned, obviously unhappy with her decision. "What do you want me to tell your mother?"

"Tell her I've had all the surprises I can take for one night."

"Angela."

"What?"

"Don't take too long."

"I'm just going to get wine," she said. "How long could that take?"

END OF EXCERPT

Booklist

About the Author

Barbara Freethy is a #1 New York Times Bestselling Author, a distinction she received for her novel, SUMMER SECRETS. Her 30 novels range from contemporary romance to romantic suspense and women's fiction. Her books have won numerous awards - she is a five-time finalist for the RITA for best contemporary romance from Romance Writers of America and her book DANIEL'S GIFT won the honor and was also optioned for a television movie.

Known for her emotional and compelling stories of love, family, mystery and romance, Barbara enjoys writing about ordinary people caught up in extraordinary adventures. Her latest series, THE WISH SERIES, is being released in 2012. A SECRET WISH, Book #1, was out in January 2012 and JUST A WISH AWAY is being released in May 2012.

Barbara has lived all over the state of California and currently resides in Northern California where she draws much of her inspiration from the beautiful bay area.

Find her on the web at:
www.barbarafreethy.com
www.facebook.com/barbarafreethybooks
www.twitter.com/barbarafreethy

18163829R00140

Made in the USA
Lexington, KY
18 October 2012